AN ARTFUL COMPROMISE

HOLLY NEWMAN

OLIVER HEBER BOOKS

PUBLISHER'S NOTE: This is a work of fiction. Names, characters, places, and incidents either are the product of the author's imagination or are used fictitiously. Any resemblance to actual persons, living or dead, business establishments, events, or locales is entirely coincidental.

Copyright ©2022 by Holly Thompson

Published by Oliver-Heber Books

0 9 8 7 6 5 4 3 2 1

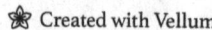 Created with Vellum

CHAPTER 1

THE POTTERY

Helena Littledean had a headache. She woke with it, for no reason she could discern. Just a little headache.

With the help of her solemn maid, Eloise, she resolutely dressed for work in a serviceable taupe-patterned dress with a brown pelisse. Not that others in the neighborhood—or the city—were to know she *worked* at Littledean Fine Porcelain. As far as the world outside the factory and her home were concerned, she acted as her father's messenger; his eyes, ears, and mouthpiece since an apoplexy left him partially paralyzed. She did not decide, she merely relayed decisions. — Or so they let the world believe.

She brushed her orange hair—for she refused to use any fancy name for what society considered a terribly unflattering hair color—and wound it into a braided coronet at the top of her head while her maid tidied her room. Despite all her smoothing, when she looked in her mirror, she saw a few hair strands insisting on independence and curling gently around her face. She sighed. The banes of her existence: wild orange hair, freckles across her nose and cheeks, and small breasts. She'd long ago learned some things can't be changed and would have to do.

She walked down the marble staircase, Dessie, her tiny black and tan toy terrier at her heels, and walked into the breakfast parlor. Her father was before her, dressed in one of his dark charcoal gray business suits as he did every day, though he seldom left the house. He sat in his Bath wheeled chair, for walking remained tiring. He'd lifted his right hand and set it on to the table, and with his left he clenched a fork, eating far more handily than he had over a year ago when he'd suffered his apoplexy.

Helena smiled lovingly at him as she sat down. "Good morning, Father," she said. "Did you sleep well last night?"

He nodded. "Wayesh," he said, which Helena knew was "Yes" in his garbled speech.

"Ear," he said, pushing a letter to her just as a footman on her other side set a tea service before her. Her father shook his head. "Ba-a."

"Bad?" she repeated to ensure she'd understood him correctly as she picked up the letter from the table. He nodded.

The letter was from Dr. Baylor, the local physician.

April 21, 1816

I regret to inform you, sir, that your accountant, Mr. Edmund Wallace, has severely broken his right wrist. I have splinted it and given him laudanum. The member will need to be kept elevated and still for several days for the swelling to subside. After that, it will be a few weeks before he has rudimentary use of that hand. I have told him when the swelling is down, he may return to work in a supervisory capacity. He is distraught at this stricture, and I know he would like to ignore it, which is why I am informing you. No writing until I say he might.

Yours, Dr. Robert Baylor

The mild pressure above her eyes invited her temples to join her headache, like an orchestra tuning for a concert. She rubbed her hand against her temples.

"Oh dear. And Mr. Bickley left four days ago for London," Helena said as their downstairs maid set a plate of food before her.

"Hu-uh?" said her father.

"I'm sorry, I forgot to tell you. Mother finished the design sketches she did for Lady Syford's service commission. He took the sketches for approval, along with samples of the new breakfast service line you suggested to our London showroom. I also asked him to meet with the showroom staff to get a sense of any new fashion trends we should consider. He said he would return before we need to leave for our trip to Devon."

"Gou, gou," her father said, nodding.

"Poor Mr. Wallace," Helena said between bites of succulent ham. "I wonder how he came to break his wrist. He is ever such a careful, fastidious man."

She cocked her head to the side. "Thankfully, it is not month-end—still, that is only a week away and from what the doctor writes, it doesn't sound like he shall be well enough then for the month end necessities."

She raised another bite of her breakfast to her lips, then stopped. "Perhaps I should remain here when you and mother go to Devon," she considered, a frown furrowing her brow.

It was not what she would wish. She'd been looking forward to the trip. She had been nowhere since the Sicily trip she took with her grandmother, her cousin Ann Hallowell, and her Aunt Catherine and her husband, Lord Candelstone, two years ago.

Her father scowled, shook his head, and became agitated, shaking his good left hand at her.

Helena pulled her attention away from the memories and back to him. "What is it?"

"Wi- Wi- carh," he got out.

"Wicar?" Helena asked. "Oh, you mean the Vicar?"

Her father nodded. His brow furrowed.

Helena waited. She knew he was concentrating on what he wanted to say.

"Skoo," he finally said, looking at her fiercely from beneath shaggy gray brows.

"Skoo? — School? The school the vicar runs?"

"Wayesh. Bo-uy wat."

Helena stared at her father.

"Bo-uy wat," he repeated.

She repeated the phase in her head, her eyes darting about as she thought about what he could mean.

After a year, she was better at understanding; however, some days were more challenging than others. Her eyes widened. "Boy, write!" she said. "You're suggesting we get a boy from the Vicar's school to write for Mr. Wallace?"

He nodded and smiled his lopsided smile.

"That's brilliant, Father!" she exclaimed, her fork clattering on to her plate.

The headache released its grip on her temples ever so slightly. She breathed deeply and brushed an errant stand of hair away from her eyes.

"What's brilliant?" asked Mrs. Littledean from the breakfast parlor doorway. A streak of clay slip had dried on her forehead from where she'd pushed her graying blond hair out of her face and her hands, though clean, showed traces of clay beneath her fingernails.

"You are up early," Helena said.

"Yes, I felt inspired this morning," her mother said as she stepped around the table to give her husband a gentle good morning hug and to drop a light kiss on his balding head. She rested her hands on her husband's shoulders. "I had the sudden idea to make a small full form statue of the design I made for Lady Syford's dinner service."

Helena nodded, as did her father. With his left hand, he patted his wife's hand where it lay on his right shoulder. When her mother formed an idea for a piece, she immediately set to work to give form to her vision. She had been known to leave the dinner table in the middle of a meal when inspiration struck.

"But tell me about my wonderful husband's brilliance," Mrs. Littledean said, gazing down affectionately at her spouse.

"He had a message this morning that Mr. Wallace broke his right wrist and cannot write for some time. I was thinking I should have to take up the ledgers; however, Father has had the idea that we can have one of the Vicar's students write the figures in the ledgers at Mr. Wallace's instructions."

Mrs. Littledean's brows rose slightly, then she smiled and nodded. "It should be a great experience for one of them." She hugged her husband again.

Helena smiled, with a smidge of envy and a wee dab of jealousy. Her heart hoped one day she, too, might find a love as encompassing as her parents shared. Her practical mind doubted that eventuality. She did not fit in anywhere. Those from trade assumed her to be society, those in society considered her too trade, with neither side bothering to discover what she was. She didn't consider herself one or the other. Who she wanted to be known as was the sculptress, Helena Littledean.

She sighed. It didn't matter. She was past what they considered marriageable age.

Her mother dropped a light kiss on her father's head.

While society frowned upon such shows of affection, Helena knew her mother had never adhered to those dictates, even if she was the daughter of a duke. She shunned her honorific *Lady* title and preferred to be known as Mrs. Littledean. Twenty-three years ago, at eighteen, she'd fallen in love with Josiah Littledean, the potter, and never looked back.

"I'll stop by the vicarage to speak with Mr. Drummond on my way home today," Helena said, already feeling left behind as her parents' attention circled about each other. She smiled again and looked down lest either of them comment on the sadness she felt certain could be seen in her eyes.

HELENA CLIMBED down from the coach in front of the rambling, sooty-red brick Littledean Fine Porcelain factory some twenty minutes later, Dessie tucked firmly under her arm. She didn't trust the little dog not to run off and get trampled in traffic.

"You can pick me up at half past two, Derek," she told the coachman. "I will visit the vicar this afternoon."

"Very good, Miss," that worthy said, deferentially nodding to her as he held the reins.

With Mr. Wallace absent, the office was still locked. It was awkward to juggle the small dog and her reticule to grasp her key, but after a moment, she opened the door and went inside. She set Dessie down once the door closed and the dog immediately raced off to survey every corner and sniff every piece of furniture. One would think she had never been in the office before when, in reality, she came nearly every day Helena did.

The front office, with its rows of shelves displaying their wares and the high clerks' desks set facing each other, front to front, felt close and smelled stale. Aside from the display of their wares, it was a plain, almost austere, business space. Rather dark, requiring lamp lighting even during the best of weather, Helena often thought the room was more a cave than a place of business.

She opened the street window shutters to let in more light and to refresh the air. On firing days, the windows had to be kept tightly latched to protect the office from the dense coal smoke that belched upward from the three massive bottle ovens, only to spread out and blanket the factory and the surrounding neighborhood.

With Mr. Wallace out and Mr. Bickley in London, that left the daily office tasks to her.

She hung her bonnet and pelisse on a hook on the wall and donned her canvas work apron before sitting at Mr. Wallace's high desk. Thankfully, it was not month-end when they tallied the ledgers, paid the staff and the merchants. Nonetheless, there were invoices to issue and, unfortunately, dunning letters to write. Those activities kept her busy.

The office stayed quiet save for the sounds of the factory and street traffic coming in through the open window. They were almost lulling sounds. Her tasks went quickly. When the side door that led into the factory courtyard opened later, she glanced at the clock on the self on the back wall. She was surprised to discover how much time had passed.

"Afternoon, Miss Littledean," said George Stringer coming into the office. "Picked up the mail. There's one wat's got a fancy frank on it, I'd say."

"Thank you, George," Helena said with a small laugh.

George presided over the casting workers, but with Mr. Bickley away, he liked to show his usefulness, hoping for a promotion from a department manager to the factory manager, a vacant position following the death of Edmund Richmond three months ago. Neither she nor Mr. Bickley thought to hurry to fill the position. Between them, they ran the factory.

The small stack of mail included a letter from the Apple Valley Mine, the clay mine owned by the Earl of Monteith, from whom they purchased most of the ball clay they mixed with kaolin clay for their high-end wares. The letter was to inform them of a price increase.

Her temples throbbed. The little headaches from the morning blossoming again. She sighed.

The price increase wouldn't beggar them. In a corner of her mind, she had been expecting it ever since they received the news of a new business manager at the mine; however, she and Mr. Bickley had hoped it would be a few more months away so they would have the chance to pay for a fourth bottle oven to be built.

Hopefully, they wouldn't need the clay from the Apple Valley Mine. A new clay seam had been discovered on the Earl of Norwalk's estate in Devon and they had invited Littledean Fine Porcelain to enjoy the first rights of purchase.

The Dowager Countess of Norwalk and Mrs. Littledean had been school friends at Mrs. Napleton's Academy for Young Ladies and had stayed in contact through the years. When the earl discovered the rich seam of ball clay on the estate, his mother insisted he contact Littledean Fine Porcelain before all the other potteries.

He was setting up his clay mine, and he invited them to Devon for consulting, and hopefully to secure a contract for the clay on good terms for both parties.

At least that was the plan, with Helena acting as interpreter for her father, allowing her mother and the Dowager Countess the opportunity to visit together. It was so hard for her father to communicate, and he had so much wisdom to share.

"Problems, Miss Littledean?"

"What?" Helena looked up. She hadn't realized George still stood in the office. "Yes. An annoying little one. Not to worry, George."

"Well, if ya needs anything with Mr. Bickley and Mr. Wallace out, I can help."

"I know, George, and I appreciated your willingness. I woke with a headache today, so even the smallest annoyance seems bigger," she said ruefully.

"Ah, I understand how that be," George said, nodding. "Yes, I do. Well then, if there be nothing else, I'll be back to the casting."

"Thank you, George," Helena said. She looked back down at the letter in front of her.

George shuffled his feet for a moment, clearly conveying to Helena his wish for more discourse. When she didn't look up again, he left the office.

Helena looked up when the door closed behind him. She slid off the high stool. She sighed again as she walked to the windows and looked out onto the street that ran before the factory.

Though Helena sometimes chaffed at not being recognized for her success with running the pottery; a part of her would not have minded selling the factory, if the price were right. She loved the business; however, she loved sculpting more. That was her passion. That was where she preferred her recognition come from.

Some days, she wondered if she was fooling herself with her deep, intrinsic belief in art.

No! Others could not take that away from her.

There was a visceral pleasure in the clay's feel. She loved shaping the damp clay with her hands, stroking a rough blob into a smooth, silken form with her fingertips. It was a sensual feeling. Just thinking about it made her shiver inside.

As an artist, she wanted to go beyond clay, to experiment with larger forms and other materials. In the evenings she studied lost wax casting for she held tight to a dream of one day producing the figure in the Clarence Wingate painting of the *Garden of Eden*—that she kept guiltily stored behind dust covers in her studio—into a life-sized bronze.

Wryly, she acknowledged her biggest obstacle to achieving her goal was her woefully scant knowledge of the male form. The painting was two dimensional and front focused—delightfully front focused, she thought, smiling as she thought about it.

She had experimented with producing the image as a smaller statue; however, her backside rendition always disappointed her.

She scrunched her nose.

She did not know why it had become so difficult. It was not like she was naïve to the male nude form. She may not have had male nudes for her sketching exercises; however, classical statuary nudes were in her grandmother's art collection and in all the museums they visited in the city. To say nothing of the classical paintings displayed. But it wasn't the same.

The back side of the male forms she created looked lifeless. She twirled an errant orange curl around her finger.

How did the blood flow, the muscles bunch and move?

Cold marble or bronze couldn't tell her that. At least, not like she'd like to see. She wanted to study the movement, too. She frowned. Women lacked the access to nude models that male artists enjoyed. It seemed unfair. Though, Helena admitted, even if there were establishments where she could sketch the nude form, her father would forbid it.

She sighed. She turned back to the high desks and her correspondence.

Though she may yearn for time to pursue her art, so long as her father lived, she would care for his legacy and ensure its continued success through price increases, absent accountants, and troublesome headaches.

"*Excuse, mademoiselle*," said a soft voice from the door into the factory.

Helena looked up. Miss Maria Velois, a French emigree and talented glaze painter, stood in the doorway.

Seeing Helena look her way. Miss Velois took a tentative step into the office. "It is permitted?" she asked tentatively. The woman was scarcely over ten years Helena's elder; however, at her temples, gray streaked her dark brown hair. Helena always wondered what lay in her past that she looked so much older than she knew her to be. She would not; however, dare ask.

"Yes, of course, come in," Helena said. She glanced at the clock. She'd been daydreaming too long. Her coachman would be by to pick her up in ten minutes. "Is something the matter?" she asked as she began straightening her papers.

"Oui, I mean, yes, sorry..." Miss Velois said, embarrassed, twisting folds of her voluminous blue apron in her fingers. "It is the new paint color Mr. Bickley calls Persian Green—though I tell him it should be Parisian Green," she said with a mischievous grin.

Helena suppressed a smile. "I'm familiar with it. It is the dominate color for the new line. It's a very soft shade."

"Yes, but it is gone."

"Gone? What do you mean, gone?"

"Hmm, all used? No more?" Miss Velois said, trying to be careful with her English.

"Oh, can't we make more?" Helena asked.

"Yes, but we don't have hmmm—" She made a writing motion with her hands. "Recipe? No—" She shook her lightly graying curls. "He call it formula," she said decisively.

Helena nodded. "And he keeps all the color formulas in his safe."

"Yes."

"I understand," Helena said. "Mr. Littledean keeps copies of all color formulae at our home, as well. I will get with him tonight to find out about this color," she assured her as she untied her apron strings and pulled the apron over her head. "Is there anything that can be painted in that line first?"

"Non, mademoiselle," Miss Velois said dolefully. "It must be first."

"So, you believe we must halt all work on the line until we have more paint?"

"Yes."

"Why didn't Mr. Humphries come and tell me this is advance?"

"That one." Miss Velois made a disgusted expression. "He eats or sleeps."

Helena raised an eyebrow at Miss Velois's vehemence. "Alright. I will bring in the color formula early tomorrow. And I will see that none of the painters are docked for the early afternoon. Now, if you'll excuse me, I have another errand I must see to today," she said, grabbing her bonnet and pelisse off the hook.

"*Oui, mademoiselle*," said Miss Velois. She bobbed a curtsey.

Helena laughed. "None of that between two working women. Off with you. I must lock up now. Enjoy your afternoon," Helena said, smiling at her, while the day long headache now throbbed in her head. She picked up Dessie from her bed and saw Miss Velois out the door. She shifted Dessie's weight in her arms as she took a last look around the office to see if she was forgetting anything, and followed behind Miss Velois, locking the door.

AT PICKERING COTTAGE, Helena sternly instructed Dessie to stay in the carriage. Dessie yipped sharply in response. Helena raised an eyebrow and shook her finger at the little dog. "None of that," she said. "I shan't be long," she added, as much to the coachman as to the dog. She hastened up the walk to the black painted door, a sharp contrast to the white-washed brick building. The two-story vicarage was too large for the cottage name; however, with its thick thatched roof with sculpted eaves on the second floor, and sculpted overhangs at the windows, it looked settled in place and not nearly as large as Helena knew it to be.

Mr. Drummond surprised Helena by answering the door to her vigorous bell jangling.

"Miss Littledean! Do come in!" he looked behind her. "Is anyone with you?"

"No, I've just left the factory."

Mr. Drummond *tut-tutted*, shaking his head. "Young ladies shouldn't be about without a chaperone," he gently reprimanded.

Helena laughed. "I shall take that as a compliment, Vicar; however, I believe you are confusing me with the gentry."

Mr. Drummond looked affronted. "Not at all, Miss Littledean. I am cognizant of your position in our society as you should be yourself. The Littledeans are well respected."

She inclined her head. "Thank you for that," she said.

Mrs. Clapham, the vicar's housekeeper, bustled toward them from the kitchen. "So delighted, Miss Littledean! I shall make tea!" she enthused.

"Please don't trouble yourself," Helena said. "I came by to have a brief word with Mr. Drummond, then I should be on my way home."

"This is not a social call? I am cast down," the vicar said playfully as he slapped one hand to his chest, his dark brown eyes twinkling.

Helena laughed, as she knew he wished her to do. "No, it is in the nature of a business call."

"Business! Then let us remove to my office. The boys should be about their reading for another twenty minutes. I always have them read toward the end of the day's lessons. I think reading can help to focus the mind, and truthfully, some of them need all the focusing I can give them," he said solemnly, then grinned.

"It is because of your students that I am here," Helena said, walking into the vicarage book-lined study.

"Oh?" Mr. Drummond said, his playfulness falling away. "Have any of them been obstreperous?"

"No, no. Nothing like that, I assure you," said Helena quickly. She sat in one of the worn oak chairs placed before his desk. She knew the vicar was quite proud of his students and would take any fault of theirs as his own.

"I have come to see if we might hire someone to assist Mr. Wallace," she said.

"Assist Mr. Wallace?" the vicar repeated as he took the seat opposite her. He gave a sharp laugh. "I've never known William Wallace to need assistance, to want assistance, or to even accept assistance."

Helena nodded. "I know. He may not have in the past; however, he will need help for the next two months at least."

The vicar leaned back in his chair, steepling his fingers against his lips. "Why?" he asked.

"He has broken his wrist, and it is his right wrist, you see. The doctor has banned him from even attempting to write until it heals."

Mr. Drummond shook his head and *tut-tutted* again. "Terrible for an accountant not to be able to attend to his ledgers."

"Precisely. That is why I'm here." She leaned forward eagerly. "Father had the idea that one or another of your students could be Mr. Wallace's amanuensis. If their handwriting is neat enough, and their mathematical skills well enough to add columns of numbers, that would be a tremendous benefit. Mother also felt it might be a wonderful experience and perhaps they might take turns, so no one misses too much school. We would pay them, of course."

Mr. Drummond stroked his chin. "It is an interesting idea, and I can see the merit for the boys and Littledean Fine Porcelain; however, how will Mr. Wallace take to it?"

"He will have no choice if he wishes to keep his position. I know that sounds harsh; however, I must think about the needs of the company."

Mr. Drummond nodded. "Let me think on it and broach it with one or two of the boys to get their feelings on it. I think we will have no lack of volunteers; the issue will be in selecting the right ones without causing undue jealousy."

"A competition, perhaps?" Helena suggested. "With essays to be read and judged by my father. They might even submit anonymously, so we might judge them for clarity of thought and penmanship."

The vicar tilted his head as he considered the idea. "That is an excellent suggestion, Miss Littledean!"

"Perhaps you can come to Tyche Manor tomorrow at four in the afternoon for tea to discuss the opportunity with my father? He might have more to offer."

The vicar hesitated. "Has his speech improved at all?"

"Sadly no; however, mother and I have become proficient at translating his meaning to others."

He laughed. "Josiah Littledean is as sharp as ever. Woe to anyone who assumes his physical frailties have diminished his mind."

Helena nodded. She rose from the chair by the desk. "Then I shall leave it to you to arrange it and we will see you tomorrow at Tyche Manor. We need to arrange everything as quickly as possible, for we are to travel to Devon next week."

He walked her to the door.

"Thank you for coming, Miss Littledean. I think this is a splendid idea."

Helena returned to the carriage in a better frame of mind than when she had entered it earlier. Better yet, that incessant pounding in her head had lessened. She could return home without causing her father or mother to worry.

CHAPTER 2
THE LADIES TAKE CHARGE

Helena wandered into her studio, the disused orangery her parents had given her for her art. On the west side of the house, it had tall windows to let in the light. Its location, facing the afternoon sun, had not been ideal for an orangery, but the space suited Helena. Late afternoon light typically streamed into the space on sunny days. However, this afternoon the sky was overcast as it had been for much of the spring. The light coming into her studio was soft, diffuse.

There was a lantern and a tinderbox on the sideboard. She opened the tinderbox but stopped, her eye catching sight of the large painting sitting on an easel in a corner near the windows. The image was completely enshrouded in a Holland cover meant for a large chair. She smiled as she contemplated the covered artwork.

A cloud of clay dust billowed into the air when she drew the Holland cover aside. She coughed and waved the dust away. It had been a long time since she'd looked at the painting; she conceded wryly. She remembered when she first saw the work of art. It had been two years ago, in Sicily, at Villa de Fiori.

She'd traveled with her cousin Ann Hallowell, her grandmother, and Lord and Lady Candelstone to Sicily during the height of the wars with Napoleon. Madness, but Sicily had been a British protectorate. Her grandmother went to view Lady Travis' art collection before she sold it, to claim first those pieces she wished to acquire. The rest would go to her uncle Aidan Nowlton's gallery in Mayfair.

Her cousin had discovered the painting and insisted Helena see it, too.

"There's a painting I want you to see. I knew when I saw it yesterday that you should like it. But I can't seem to find it," Ann said.

Helena took a lantern off the table and walked toward her cousin. "What's its subject?"

"It's a picture of a young man, but it isn't in the portrait or figure painting stacks." Ann turned her head to look at Helena. "It's a picture of a man standing in a garden."

The sly humor in her cousin's expression convinced Helena that indeed the painting was worth discovering. "If it has a garden, perhaps it's among the landscapes."

"Or among the religious paintings," Ann said, moving over to the stack of large landscapes.

"Religious?" Helena laughed. "You seem uncertain, cuz. I thought grandmother taught you better than that," she teased.

Ann laughed. "You shall see my confusion when I find it.... Ah, here it is." She turned toward her cousin. "Stand directly in front and hold the lantern high while I move these other paintings aside."

Helena cocked an eyebrow, but humoring her cousin, did as she asked.

"Oh, my!" she exclaimed when Ann slid three canvases

away. She sank down on her knees before the painting, oblivious to the dusty floor. "Oh, dear!" Her eyes wide, she set the lantern on the floor beside her, then reached out tentatively, as if to touch the painting. Catching herself, she hastily drew her hand back, resting it against the Indian muslin fichu at her throat.

Ann laughed. "I knew you should like it."

"I am uncertain that <u>like</u> is the correct word," Helena breathed. "And I'm not at all certain if I should look at it or blush and avert my eyes. He takes my breath away."

The awe in her cousin's voice made Ann smile. "He?" she teased.

"I mean <u>it</u>. The painting, of course." Helena glanced up at her cousin, then back at the painting.

Deep shadows and the bright golden sunlit colors of the garden battled to claim the figure in the painting, much like a biblical war betwixt evil and good. The artist had portrayed that young man—the subject of that war—as naked in the center of the battle, a half-eaten apple in his hand. Amazing bright gold eyes shone from beneath straight, dark, almost black brows with an independent light and self-assuredness that belied the young man's unclothed state. Thick, dark hair, unfashionably long, waved across his brow and down his neck. Broad shoulders stressed his narrow hips and ropey muscles. And though the young man could not have been over eighteen or nineteen, he wore calm maturity like an invisible mantle. Technically, the painting was magnificently rendered; but more than that, the artist had captured magic and power with his brushes and pots of paints.

"Oh, you are a cruel woman, Ann Hallowell, to show me this painting. Not only is it a beautiful painting, but...."

Ann kneeled beside her. "But so is its subject," she finished for her cousin.

After the workmen had crated the painting, she'd

surreptitiously put her direction on the crate. She'd
not told anyone what she'd done, not even Ann. When
it arrived at her home some months later, her parents
had laughed at her actions, but kept her secret. Ann
had questioned her in letters, but Helena never made
a direct comment. For a time, there was speculation
within the family about the painting, but eventually
that too died away.

The painting spoke to her as a sculptor and as a
woman. She discovered the artist was Clarence
Wingate. The youngest son of the third Duke of
Ellinbourne. She'd read he died a few years ago in
Greece. His paintings were in high demand. But she'd
never heard of an artwork like this from him. There
was a sensual earthiness to the painting that touched
Helena's soul. Every man she met paled compared to
this man, a fantasy man in a Garden of Eden painting.
Sometimes she wished Ann had never shown her the
picture. But she knew, if she'd never seen it, she would
always feel as if she'd missed something.

She stared at the painting and smiled. Something
about it calmed her. Here was the epitome of her
dream man. She loved his smile and how it lit his entire face. He enjoyed life and faced it with confidence
—far more confidence than she felt. She envied him
that.

The afternoon light faded.

She sighed. Time for supper. She tossed the Holland cover back over the painting and left the room.

"ARE you sure you wish to go with me to the factory?"
Helena asked her mother. She turned to gaze into one
of the pier glass mirrors that flanked the heavy oak

front door as she settled her straw bonnet on her head and tied its peach ribbons in a neat bow.

Helena did not concern herself with fashion; however, she did like this straw bonnet. It drew her attention when she first saw it in the millinery shop window because of its lightweight construction, but she found she quite liked how it looked on her. It somehow complemented her orange hair and rather sharp features. She'd received several compliments when she'd worn it to Sunday services.

Her mother came up behind her and placed her hands on her shoulders. "Yes, I do. Before we leave on our trip, I would like to see how they are doing with my designs. I don't know how long we will be gone, and I believe a judicious eye over their activities will remind the workers of our expectations. In particular, I want to see the glazing done on the new service. I would not have thought them to be running out of glaze. Mr. Humphries should have seen that there was plenty."

Helena laughed shortly. "Not to be spreading gossip; however, Miss Velois said Mr. Humphries spends his time eating or sleeping."

Her mother looked at her sharply.

Helena shrugged apologetically. "I admit I have not monitored that area as much as other departments, for they continuously turn out skilled, beautiful work."

Her mother's lips compressed into a tight line. "That may be. Still, I wish to oversee the glaze color mixing myself. And to have a word with Mr. Humphries."

Helena nodded. "I understand that desire."

She picked up her reticule from the hallway table. "Come Dessie," she called to her dog. Her pet came

running up, panting excitedly. Helena laughed as she
bent to pick her up. The dog quivered with excitement. "You would think going to the factory would be
blasé for her right now," she said as she straightened
and settled Dessie in the crook of her arm.

Her mother chuckled. "For dogs, it never gets old,"
she observed. She scratched the top of Dessie's head
before proceeding Helena to their carriage.

～

"THAT'S ODD," Helena said as she descended from the
carriage after her mother. "There is a lantern lit in the
office."

She hurried around her mother to the front door.
She depressed the latch, surprised to find it click. She
pushed the door open. A man stood before the cupboard that housed the accounting books. The doors
were open. He jumped back and slammed the doors
as he turned to face the entrance.

"Mr. Wallace! What are you doing here?" Helena
asked.

She set Dessie on the floor and crossed the room
to where the accountant stood with his right arm
heavily splinted and in a sling. Her mother followed
her, a heavy frown creasing her brow.

"Dr. Baylor specifically said you were to rest for
several days to get the swelling to subside. Look at
your fingers! There are as fat as sausages!" Helena exclaimed. She stood, her hands on her hips, as she
looked him up and down.

"There is work to be done," the short, stout man
said, his voice quavering. He tried to smile cajolingly,
but to Helena, he looked more like a conniving lep-
rechaun. Her eyes narrowed.

"Yes, but you can't do it yet. I also read the note from Dr. Baylor," Mrs. Littledean scolded. "We need you to return to the office by the time we leave for Devon next week. If you do not rest that arm, the doctor will not let you do that. And what have you under your left arm?" she asked, seeing him holding one of the account books partially behind his back.

He edged back against one of the high desks and set the book down. "Just an account book."

"And what do you think you could do with that account book with your arm trussed up and your hand so swollen?"

"Account books can't be left unattended," he said.

"And I attended to this one yesterday," Helena said, picking it up off the desk. She walked around him and put it back in the ledger cupboard, closing the doors.

"You?"

She looked at him quizzically. "Yes, me. Why are you surprised?"

"I — well, I—"

"Mr. Wallace," Mrs. Littledean said, "Do you believe Mr. Littledean knows all facets of Littledean Fine Porcelain?"

"Yes! Of course," the man said. He fidgeted with his sling, nervously readjusting the support on his right arm. "But—" His voice trailed off.

"But what?"

"But he hasn't been here since — since—" He looked down.

"Since his apoplexy?"

"Yes." He looked up then, almost defiantly. "A lot has happened in a year."

Mrs. Littledean nodded. "And our daughter and Mr. Bickley have kept him well informed."

"Have the revenues not increased this past year?" Helena asked. "Mr. Wallace, I shouldn't have to remind you that my father's impairments are physical, not mental."

Mrs. Littledean stepped back and crossed her arms in front of her waist. "You are not to touch the account books until Dr. Baylor says you may. Give me your key to the office," she directed, every inch a duke's daughter.

Helena smiled secretly at her mother.

"What? No!" Mr. Wallace said, clapping his good hand over his waistcoat pocket.

"You are a good and loyal employee, Mr. Wallace, and as a loyal employee I do not trust you not to come back here to work while we are not here," Mrs. Littledean said.

"But it's almost month's end!"

"Yes, we know, and Mr. Littledean has a plan. He is getting you a temporary assistant. One of the vicar's students," Helena said.

He gasped. "What? No! I don't like anyone touching these books," he said, glaring slightly at Helena. "And a child? Impossible!"

"You must make it possible," she responded earnestly. "They will be your writing hand working under your direction."

"I'm afraid we must insist," Mrs. Littledean said.

"A grubby schoolboy splattering ink and dirty hands on my books? Their writing will be indecipherable and their mathematics impossible. No, no, no," Mr. Wallace protested as he looked over at the closed cabinet.

"There is to be a competition among the boys for the best penmanship and mathematical ability. My father is to be the judge," Helena explained.

"You don't have a choice," Mrs. Littledean reiterated. "The key, please?"

Mr. Wallace looked from one woman to the other. He reached into his pocket and pulled out the key. He held it out. Helena took it from him.

"Thank you, Mr. Wallace," she said. She put the large key into her reticule. "Dr. Baylor said in his note that you need to keep your arm elevated for a few days to encourage that swelling to go down.

"As I said before, we want you to return to work before we leave for Devon, and that cannot happen if the doctor does not see improvement," Helena's mother explained. "I hope you have not injured it more by your foolishness today."

"I will get your new assistant familiar with the factory and the ledgers before you return. Have no worries there," Helena promised.

Mr. Wallace nodded and walked to the door, his shoulders slumping. As he opened it, Dessie ran toward the opening.

"Dessie!" Helena called out. "Come back here!" She ran forward to catch her little dog. "You cannot go with Mr. Wallace," she reprimanded her. She looked up at Mr. Wallace. "Take care of that arm and we will see you again soon."

"Yes, Miss," Mr. Wallace said glumly.

The door closed behind him.

"That actually went better than I thought it would," Mrs. Littledean said.

"Probably because he felt guilty for being caught here," Helena said as she set Dessie back on the floor.

Her mother laughed. "Most likely."

"And I love seeing the duke's daughter appear."

Her mother scrunched up her nose in an un-duke's daughter way. "I suppose I was a trifle severe."

"No more so than he needed to hear. And you can carry it off. I never could have done that!"

Her mother sighed as she shrugged. "Some things are more difficult to unlearn," she confessed wryly. "It is not something I am particularly proud of; however, it has its uses."

Mrs. Littledean walked to the factory courtyard door. "Now, to see to the glaze color mixing."

"I'll be checking the ledgers for what is due today. We should receive a big load of coal for the next glost firing."

Her mother nodded. "I hope the lack of glaze will not delay that firing unduly," she said. "I'll check into that as well," she said as she opened the door.

HELENA and her mother did not leave the pottery until nearly four in the afternoon. With both of them there and Mr. Bickley and Mr. Wallace not around, it seemed everyone wanted to speak to them and nearly all the topics were complaints.

"We shall be late for tea," Lady Littledean observed as the carriage turned off of the city streets toward the country where they lived two miles away.

"I hope the vicar has not come by yet. He specifically asked me about father's speech yesterday afternoon. I think the man is afraid he won't understand him," Helena said.

Mrs. Littledean sighed. "I'll own few can—other than us—and the footman Henry. And how is it that Henry can readily understand him? I do not know, but he seems to. It has taken Wolversham, his valet, who is most often in his company, the longest time to gain understanding."

"He seems to do much better in that regard of late," Helena offered.

"Yes, but I am glad it is Henry who will accompany us rather than Wolversham."

"I thought the countess advised against bringing our servants and instead said we should make use of theirs?"

"Yes, she has, as that will help us travel faster than with a large retinue; still, I feel more comfortable having a man with us who can understand your father."

Helena acknowledged that truth. "How did the color glaze mixing go?"

"Miss Velois did most of the mixing."

"I quite like her," Helena said.

"I do, too. Mr. Humphries tried to tell her she was making the glaze wrong, and that she should double the amount. I watched her. She is a meticulous woman. I told him the glaze could spoil if we make too much was at once. It could develop a skin and risk the deposit of large particles. Of course, the truth of the correctness of the color mixing will come with the glost firing."

"When we return from Devon, I want to spend more time in that area of the factory," Helena said. "Mr. Bickley and I have left that department alone, as all their work is exquisite."

Mrs. Littledean nodded. "That is a good idea. I believe you will find Miss Velois is the one who actually runs the department on a daily basis. Mr. Humphries is a figurehead. — We need to speak to Mr. Littledean about him," she said as the carriage turned into the drive leading to Tyche Manor.

"Oh dear," Helena said, looking out the carriage window. "Mr. Firkins has come to call."

Mrs. Littledean leaned across Helena to look out the window. "Looks like he arrived just in time for tea." She settled back against the cushions. "I thought you liked Mr. Firkins."

"I do, but not in the way he wishes me to—or rather not in the way his *father* wishes me to," Helena archly clarified.

Mrs. Littledean laughed and patted her daughter's hand. "Old Mr. Firkins is looking for an economical way to acquire Littledean Fine Porcelain. He has been hinting at a merger with your father for years."

"And what could be a cheaper acquisition than one gained in a marriage between the heirs of two potteries?" Helena asked in a suffering tone.

"Neither your father nor I look to see you wed to Mr. Firkins unless you wish to be. I am curious, however. What has given you such a dislike? As children, you were ever in each other's pockets."

Helena shook her head. "Tibault Firkins has no say, and no opinions other than those his father gives him. I should as well be married to the elder Firkins as the younger. He'd probably instruct his son on what to do in our bedroom if I were to marry him! Put your hand here, not there. Do this, not that."

"Helena!" her mother exclaimed, trying to sound shocked. She turned her head to hide her silent laugh, but Helena saw it.

"See, you can imagine it, too, else you would not have laughed," Helena said earnestly.

"And I will grant you that Mr. Firkins, the elder, would likely pass out to hear you talk so. Where you got this blunt speech, I don't know."

"Grandmother," Helena said.

"Ah," said her mother, sadly shaking her head. "There is truth there."

The carriage rounded the curve before the front door. Mr. Firkins waited on the doorstep, their butler standing next to him.

"Chin up," instructed Mrs. Littledean. "Pretend you haven't known Mr. Firkins since you both wore children's long gowns. Treat him instead with the same polite formality that I know you will show the Earl of Norwalk."

Helena looked over at her mother as the carriage drew to a halt. "Like the granddaughter of a duchess?" she asked, ignoring the twinge of an ache at acting like what she fears—an aristocrat.

Her mother arched an eyebrow as she smiled. "Precisely," she said as the groomsman let down the steps.

Helena knew her mother did not know how those mannerisms, coming from others, had hurt her.

Mrs. Littledean moved past her daughter to descend first, but stopped at the door, one foot on the step, as she turned back to face Helena. "On second thought," she said softly, their bonnet brims touching, "like others *expect* a Duchess to be. No one would call your grandmother a *normal* duchess," she said ruefully.

Helena laughed, the aching twinge bursting like a bubble in the bath.

"Mr. Firkins!" Mrs. Littledean exclaimed; her hand held out as she walked toward him. "What a pleasant surprise. Have you come to tea with us?"

Mr. Firkins took her gloved hand in his and bowed over it. "Yes, Mrs. Littledean, if you would have me as a visitor for your daughter."

"I should, but the question is, will she?" Mrs. Littledean returned, pulling her hand free from his.

Mr. Firkins looked confused. "What? — Oh, you

are teasing me, Mrs. Littledean. Oh yes. Ha ha. Very good," he said, nodding, his head bobbing.

Helena felt sorry for him. He had no notion that what her mother spoke was the truth.

"Mr. Firkins," she murmured as she came up beside him. In truth, he was a well set up young man. Handsome in an ordinary way. Light brown hair, brown eyes, smooth complected, well built without being muscular. And he eschewed London fashion trends, which gave him extra points from Helena. But she just could not get excited about being around him. They had known each other for years. Maybe that was it, too much familiarity, like the brother she never had. She knew that several young ladies at the regional assemblies had their speculative eyes on him.

"Miss Littledean," he returned. He bowed over her hand, holding it longer than necessary.

The slight scent of cinnamon distracted Helena. She bounced lightly on the balls of her feet. "You are in luck, Mr. Firkins," she said, smiling as she pulled her hand away to loosen the ribbons of her bonnet. "Cook has made cinnamon cakes for tea."

"Your cook's cinnamon cakes. Now that brings back childhood memories," Mr. Firkins acknowledged, straightening.

"I wonder if she has added any fruit?" Helena said.

"Probably not," her mother said. "Nothing is in season yet." She turned back to address their butler. "Sutton, has the Vicar arrived yet?"

"He has, indeed, ma'am. He and the master are in the library."

"Oh dear," Mrs. Littledean said, hurrying to remove her hat and pelisse.

"Not to worry, madame. I sent young Henry in with the refreshments tray, and he hasn't come out yet.

He is likely ensuring the good vicar understands the master. I have heard laughter."

"Laughter?!" Helena and her mother exchanged pleased glances.

"Yes, ma'am."

"Well, then, we'll have tea—with cinnamon cakes," she said with a nod in Helena's direction, "—in the drawing room. Please tell Mr. Littledean and Vicar Drummond we should like them to join us."

"Yes, ma'am," Sutton said, bowing.

Mrs. Littledean led the way to their drawing room, a fairly small room by drawing room standards; however, done up in the first stare of elegance. Light blue walls with white millwork trim lent the room a peaceful air. The drapes were a darker steel blue with a shimmery sheen. There was a glass door along the back wall that led out to a slate terrace and gardens below. Everything about the room claimed understated elegance. It was Helena's favorite room for reading and letter writing.

"Now then, Mr. Firkins," said Mrs. Littledean as she sat down in her favorite chair near the fireplace and twitched the fabric of her skirts into place. "What brings you to Tyche Manor today?"

Mr. Firkins waited for Helena to sit down. "My father has heard that Mr. Wallace is incapacitated and wishes to know if there is any way we might help Littledean Fine Porcelain in its time of need."

"Time of need?" Helena repeated.

Mr. Firkins shifted his body to face Helena. They were seated at either ends of a blue jacquard sofa.

"Yes. Father has heard of Mr. Wallace's unfortunate accident. He would like to offer one of his clerks to do your accounting in Mr. Wallace's absence."

"That didn't take long," Mrs. Littledean observed.

Helena nodded as she laughed. "Now that is a novel notion for getting access to a competitor's books," she said wryly.

Pink color climbed Mr. Firkins' neck to his cheeks. "No! No! Father would not — I mean—"

"Yes, he would," returned Helena.

"Well, it is his profound wish that we will someday wed," Mr. Firkins said, pulling on his coat collar. "And naturally, would want to understand your dowry."

Sutton carried in a tea tray and set it on a nearby table.

"I have told you before, we would not suit," Helena said gently as her mother poured tea.

"You could change your mind," Mr. Firkins suggested plaintively.

Helena sighed, shrugged, and looked up at the ceiling for a moment. She looked back at him. "Our society considers you the matrimonial catch of the local assemblies. And there are many eligible young ladies in attendance this season. You have your pick."

"Father says—" Mr. Firkins began as Mrs. Littledean handed him a teacup.

"I'm sure we all know what your father says and wants, Mr. Firkins," Mrs. Littledean said as he took the cup from her. "But what does Tibault Firkins want?" she asked.

"Me?" he squeaked, looking between Helena and Mrs. Littledean.

"Yes," Helena said. She sipped her tea. "What does Mr. Firkins, the younger, want?"

"To make my father happy, of course," he returned.

Helena shook her head. "I understand that, just as I wish to make my parents happy, but I still have my own wants and dreams. What about yours?"

He looked confused. Just then, the door to the

parlor opened to admit Mr. Littledean and Mr. Drummond. Mr. Littledean held a sheaf of papers in his hand.

"There you are!" Mrs. Littledean exclaimed. "I've been wondering if you would join us," she said.

"We have been going over the submissions from my students," Mr. Drummond said.

Mr. Littledean nodded and sat in the matching chair to his wife's. Mr. Drummond took a chair at the other end of the sofa.

Helena helped her mother serve them tea and a cinnamon cake.

"Exquisite," Mr. Drummond said after his first bite of cinnamon cake.

"Thank you. We will pass your enjoyment on to cook. I will say, however, they are even better with fruit in them. Mr. Littledean is partial to them with mulberries."

"Wayesh," said Mr. Littledean, his eyes alight.

"So, tell us about the submissions," Helena said. "Do you have potential candidates to assist Mr. Wallace?"

Her father nodded. He waved his left handing holding the papers at Mr. Drummond.

"I had five students submit essays and do mathematical exercises," Mr. Drummond said, nodding in Helena's direction. "I asked them not to sign their papers; however, I made a mark on the back of each, so I would know who submitted which paper."

"So that the name of the students could not be influential in the choice?"

"Precisely."

"Well done, sir. Well done."

"So has a winner come out of this exercise?"

"Yes, one has; and I'll admit, it is not who I would

have considered when you first proposed this to me, Miss Littledean; however, on consideration, I think he is ideal."

"Do we know him?

"What is this submission about?" Mr. Firkins asked, his brow furrowed in confusion.

"A student to write for Mr. Wallace."

"What?"

"Rather than trying to replace Mr. Wallace, which would be difficult, even for as short a time as that, we have come to another solution. The doctor said Mr. Wallace can supervise, he just cannot write. Father had the idea of getting one of the vicar's students to write what Mr. Wallace needs him to.

"A child writing in your ledger books? My father will not like that."

"And what has you father to do with Littledean Fine Porcelain ledger books?" Helena demanded. Her brows drew together, making her narrow face appear sharper.

Her mother frowned at her.

Before Mr. Firkin could answer, Mr. Drummond continued.

"Walton Michael Smythe will assist Mr. Wallace at Littledean for the next couple of months. It is perfect timing, as next term Mr. Smythe will attend Eton, per his maternal grandfather's wish."

Mr. Firkins snorted. "A Smythe at Eton? Hardly."

Helena frowned at Mr. Firkins' attitude to the Smythes. Walton Smythe's father, Robert Smythe, owned a carting company and was an investor in the canals, which had become crucial for the transportation of fragile pottery. He and his wife had six children, Walton being the third child and the only one to display a marked interest in learning.

Mr. Drummond looked at Mr. Firkins. "He has already been accepted. The boy is quite bright. While the studies at Eton are more on the classics, young Mr. Smythe hopes to one day read law."

Mr. Firkins shook his head. "Father will not like this turn of events."

"Then I suggest you hasten home to tell him," said Helena archly.

Mr. Firkins failed to hear her sarcasm. "Yes, I think I should," he said earnestly. He set his teacup down and rose to his feet.

"I thank you, Mrs. Littledean, for your hospitality." He bowed, his expression a study of concern and confusion.

"I'll show you to the door," Helena said.

"No need. I know my way. Thank you again," he said as he walked out.

Helena shook her head in wonder as she watched him leave. She turned to look at first her mother, then her father. "Must I suffer him as a suitor?"

Mrs. Littledean laughed. "We have never pushed you to Mr. Firkins."

"But isn't Mr. Firkins a fine catch?" asked Mr. Drummond. "I have often wondered why you and young Firkins have not made a match yet. He is very attentive to you after services."

"I enjoyed Tibault Firkins as my childhood friend. Then he went away to school, and I find this Tibault Firkins who has returned is not the person I knew."

"He has grown up."

"Yes, but he has no thoughts of his own. Everything is 'Father says' this and 'Father says' that."

"Miss Littledean, the bible tells us a young person should listen to their parents," Mr. Drummond admonished.

Helena closed her eyes as she sighed heavily.

"Wi—car," Mr. Littledean suddenly said. His lips were compressed in as straight a line as the frozen muscles on have his face would allow. "Hena an Fuur —kens, no," he said, shaking his head. "No lou—fa daar. No mar-aj wih-ow lou-fa."

"Thank you, Father," Helena said, touched at her father's vehemence.

Mr. Drummond looked lost.

"My husband said, *Helena and Firkins, no. No love there. No marriage without love.*" Mrs. Littledean translated for the vicar.

Mr. Drummond set his teacup down. "I see," he said carefully. "In my life observations, I've seen love to be something few can afford."

"Yes," Mrs. Littledean agreed. "But if you can find it, you are so much the richer."

"Excuse my plain speaking, Mrs. Littledean, but Miss Littledean is not likely to have an extensive selection of young men available to fall in love with."

"Which is why we shall journey to London soon. In her last letter, my mother hinted various cousins may soon get married."

"She did?" Helena said.

"Yes. You know your grandmother is full of machinations. If she says there will be nuptials, I'm sure there will be, and we will celebrate with the family."

"Ta Lon-on!" Mr. Littledean proclaimed, raising his right hand in a cheer.

Helena laughed. "To London!" she said, mimicking her father's cheer. "—after Devon," she added.

Mrs. Littledean's eyes twinkled. She nodded. "After Devon."

CHAPTER 3

MANNION HALL

"Excuse me, my lord."

Tom Winsted looked up from the surveyor's map spread out on the old oak table in the Mannion Hall estate office. He turned toward the stately, quiet voice of Beasom, the butler. Beasom stood by the door; his white-gloved hands folded patiently in front of him. Tom looked back at his employer. The Earl of Norwalk did not look up.

Dressed in shirtsleeves and dun-colored waistcoat, his brown jacket discarded across a chair, the earl sat with one hip on the table, his other leg splayed out casually before him as he continued studying the map location of the field they had been discussing. The only sign that the earl even heard the interruption existed in a new furrow carved between his black-winged brows. The furrow gave his already strong features a satyr cast. Tom glanced back at the butler standing by the door. The elderly retainer stood calmly, unperturbed by the earl's failure to immediately recognize his presence. Tom had only worked for the Earl of Norwalk for five months; however, he didn't think he'd ever be able to stand so calmly before the earl as Beasom did.

A large orange tabby cat rose from his square of sunlight at the edge of the table, stretched, and walked over to sit in the middle of the map.

The earl laughed softly. "Down, Foster," he said as he picked up the cat and set him on the floor. He turned back to studying the map with its new surveyor notes.

"Tom, I'm going to grant Coos Field to Joseph Calder in exchange for the ball clay seam we discovered at the base of Norwalk Hill. I remember we let Coos Field go fallow last year, so it's in good shape, but it's too late in the season to be planted with a grain crop." Norwalk's deep, quiet voice rumbled out of his chest. He rapped the field location on the map with his index finger. "He may plant Swedish turnips in the field this year. The turnips will provide fodder for the animals next winter. He'll have to be content with that for this season, and I think he will be. It's a good trade for him," he said as he straightened and looked up at his young estate steward.

Turned full-force in his direction, the earl's guinea-gold gaze disconcerted Tom. He blinked. "Yes —" he began. His voice squeaked like a lad in short coats. He felt a warm blush rise from this neck to stain his cheeks. He cleared his throat and swallowed. "Yes, my lord," he finally managed, his head bobbing. He fumbled for his quill. It flipped over, spattering black ink across his fingers and the open account book. He swiftly looked up at the earl to see if he'd noticed his clumsiness, but the earl was not attending him. Self-consciously, Tom tucked his ink-stained hands behind his back as he stared at the earl.

"Beasom?" the earl inquired, finally looking over at the patiently waiting butler.

"The mail is in," the butler said.

The earl shook his head, frowning. "Is there something important in the mail? Didn't you bring it?" he asked.

"No, my lord. Her ladyship received similar mail and when she read hers, she insisted I come to get you. I gather she wishes to see your expression when you read *your* correspondence."

The Earl's frowned deepened. It bracketed his lips and pulled his black brows together again for a moment. Then he sighed and straightened as he ran a hand through his wavy black hair. "Very well," he said, nodding. "Probably more about my cousin Redinger's marriage. Tell my mother I will be there directly."

The butler bowed. "Very good, my lord," he said, then turned and left, the estate room door closing it behind him with a soft click.

The earl turned back to the map on the desk.

"Do you want me to come back tomorrow, my lord?" Tom asked.

The cat jumped back up on the table.

"Hmm?" The earl turned toward Tom, the deep creases in his forehead smoothing out. "Oh. No, Tom. I want to go over the planting schedules yet today. I'll be back," he said. He gave the cat one long pet, then grabbed his jacket and shrugged into it.

Tom had heard from former schoolmates that the first stare of elegance in London was jackets made so tight their owners had to be helped into them. That might be so for some, but not for the earl, he thought as he watched Norwalk straighten his cuffs. The earl's broad shoulders and athletic build didn't need artifice to look elegant, Tom decided. He squared his slight shoulders. His friends might brag about their fancy London positions, but Tom would wager a guinea that he'd secured the best situation.

The earl strode toward the estate room door where he paused and turned back to look at Tom. "You may wish to use this time to re-enter your notes and figures on a new page in your account book," he suggested, his lips curving up into a faint smile.

Tom blushed.

The cat jumped off the table and followed the earl.

OUTSIDE THE ESTATE OFFICE, Adam, the Earl of Norwalk, let his brief smile vanish. He quickly walked down the length of the gallery toward the main block of Mannion Hall, the orange tabby cat trotting behind him. Tall mullion windows on the south wall begged for the afternoon sun. Jewel-toned carpets underfoot softened the oak floor and his heavy tread. The legions of portraits crowding the long expanse of the linenfold paneling looked down on him as he strode past. In the three years he'd possessed the Norwalk title, Adam had yet to shake the feeling that every relation he passed frowned on him as he passed them, just as his father had frowned on his only surviving son.

When he crossed the vaulted and trussed great hall, a young footman dressed in gray and green Norwalk livery ran before him to throw open the parlor door. Adam walked quickly past him into the room. The cat ducked in after him before the footman could close the door again.

His mother lounged on a pink-striped settee; a brightly colored India print shawl draped over her legs. She looked up as he stormed into the room and smiled mischievously. She held her hand up to him.

"Darling! You came! I wasn't sure you would."

"What is this all about? Why wouldn't you let Beasom bring me my letter?"

"Because, though I don't know what your letter says, I can guess, as I have had an interesting letter from my sister, Suzanne. Your letter is from Miles."

"Miles?"

"Yes, you remember him, don't you? The cousin you used to do everything with over the summers? The one who is a duke now?" the countess teased; her eyebrows arched high over her expressive amber eyes.

Adam's lips quirked upward. "Enough. I was merely questioning the sender, as Miles is not much for letter writing."

"Neither are you."

He inclined his head in acknowledgement. "Let me see this letter that you are so anxious to learn about. I told Tom Winsted I would be back soon. We have more estate matters to discuss."

"Are you going to build a new cidery this year?"

"That is in consideration. It will depend how the fruit sets—or doesn't. It's been a chilly spring."

"Oh, it will. I am certain of it," said the marchioness calmly as she held out his letter to him.

"I need to discuss with Tom the upcoming visit from the potter, Josiah Littledean. If he wants as much ball clay from that seam we discovered as he stated in his letter, that will go a long way to pulling the estate out of the river tick," he said as he took the letter from her and slid a finger beneath the ducal seal to open it.

"I am so glad I suggested you contact Littledean Fine Porcelain. I haven't seen Lady Elizabeth since before you were born, though we have kept in correspondence through the years. I am looking forward to her visit while you gentlemen conduct business," his mother said.

"I was thinking they could stay in the west wing," Adam said.

"The west wing?" She shook her head. "No. That wing has been closed for years. It is not fit for guests, to say nothing of its distance from the main part of the house. Why the west wing? I hope you are not thinking of having them stay there as he is in trade?" the dowager countess protested. "That I will not countenance."

Adam felt a slight heat rise in his neck. That *had* played into his suggestion, and as she called him on it, he realized that is what his father would have done— if not insist they stay in the village to keep the stain of trade far away. As much as he tried to rise above all his father had been, he too often aped his actions.

"No. I'm not as familiar with the house condition as I am of the estate," he said, irritated with himself. "May I count on you to make the appropriate arrangements, then?" he asked.

"Of course, dear," she said.

He nodded and looked down at the letter he held.

~

April 30, 1816

Versely Park

Dear Adam,

If the family gossip lines of communication are working at speed, you have no doubt heard that our cousin, Sebastian Redinger, has been married by special license to Miss Julia Quesinberry, Lord Berry's niece. Why special license? Not for any ruinous reasons. But that is a tale best told over a pint of ale.

I wouldn't mind a marriage by special license either, for I have found my Duchess and am eager to claim her. However, as the aunts and my mother would be horrified if I did a special license nuptial, the banns will be posted this Sunday.

Her name is Ann Hallowell, the daughter of the late Mr. and Mrs. Graham and Maria Hallowell, grand-daughter of the Dowager Duchess of Malmsby.

Why this woman before all others? There are a dozen reasons, the chief one being I have fallen in love. She makes me laugh.

There will be an engagement ball in London in six weeks—the aunts and mother insisted. You will come, of course. Invite to follow.

Yours, with cousinly regards,

Miles Wingate

6th Duke of Ellinbourne

P.S. I have a lead on THE painting.

He skimmed it, then passed it to her. "So, Miles is getting leg shackled. Bound to happen. I will send him my congratulations."

His mother read the letter, then set in down in her lap and looked at Adam quizzically.

"I'm surprised that his postscript did not have you packing your portmanteau and hastening off to London."

"What postscript?"

His mother looked at him reprovingly. "You did not read your cousin's letter completely."

Adam frowned dismissively. "My mind is on other things."

"I am aware, and I feel I must reassure you; you are a much better landholder than ever your father was, God rest his soul."

The Earl snorted as he sat down in the chair next to her settee. He ignored her comment.

His father had nearly run the estate into penury, and not from gambling or any other vice. He was always investing in one or another money-making scheme, none of which came to fruition. But he had an arrogant faith that the next one would be the one to turn the fortunes around. Luckily, his mother had her own funds, and had a shrewd head for investments. While her husband continually lost funds, she continually gained them. A fact she never boasted about or otherwise did anything to cause Adam's father embarrassment; however, due to spousal laws, he knew about it, even if he couldn't touch any of her money. He had been angered and embarrassed that a woman—his own wife—could invest better than he. That drove him to try that much harder.

Adam took the letter back from her with ill grace and read it again, slowly.

I have a lead on THE painting.

"What?"

Flashes of hot and cold tore through him. He surged out of the chair. Holding the letter in one hand, he smacked it with the back of his other hand with a resounding whack. "A lead on the painting? A lead?"

During summer visits to his grandfather's ducal Ellinbourne estate, he and his male cousins, Miles Wingate and Sebastian Redinger, used to swim naked in a pond at the edge of the apple orchard. One day, before he got dressed again, Adam grabbed an apple off a nearby apple tree to munch. His uncle, Clarence Wingate, had been with them, leaning against a tree, sketching while they swam, laughing and joking with them.

His uncle said, with the apple in his hand, he looked the epitome of Adam in the garden of Eden. He and his cousins laughed.

Little did he know that his uncle would take the sketch he had made of him that day and turn it into a large oil painting.

He paced the room, then turned back. "What does this mean? Is Miles playing a May game with me?"

"Really, Adam, that is beneath you," his mother said with gentle humor. "Consider who the letter is from. That would not be Miles even on his worst day!"

Adam's fist closed tightly around the letter; his knuckles white. He closed his eyes as he took in a deep breath, then let it out. "My apologies, Mother. You are correct. But why doesn't he tell me what he knows?"

"He says he has a lead. A lead differs from knowing."

Adam's head dropped in acquiescence. He took a deep breath. He was overreacting. But he clearly remembered the day his uncle showed the painting to the family.

He'd been down from the university between terms. The family had gone to his grandfather's to celebrate something—he could not remember what. The extended family had been there as well. After dinner one evening, his Uncle Clarence had said he wanted to show the family what he considered his greatest artwork yet. He'd led them into the gold parlor, where he had a large painting covered with one of his grandmother's shawls on an easel in the middle of the room.

When he had their attention, he'd grinned and whisked the shawl away.

Silence for a heartbeat. Then his female cousins squealed and looked away, hiding behind fans and handkerchiefs. His male cousins laughed, his aunts gasped, and his uncles' voices rose in protest. Red climbed Adam's neck and suffused his face. Uncle Samuel picked up the shawl from where Uncle Clarence had discarded it and threw it back over the painting.

"What?" Uncle Clarence had demanded. "You are all philistines!" he'd said when they tried to explain their outrage. He'd grabbed the painting off the easel and stalked out of the room.

Adam only saw the painting once more after that. He went to his uncle's room the next day to buy the painting from him. The painting once again stood on an easel, now uncovered. He glared at it. He admitted it was his uncle's best work. It forced someone to stare at it, to take it in.

He, however, didn't want to appreciate his uncle's talent. He wanted to destroy any evidence the painting had ever existed. His uncle wouldn't give him the painting. He was ever too short of funds for that kind of generosity. Adam offered to buy it. His uncle refused to sell it as he knew Adam's intention by his manner.

Clarence smarted at the family's reaction to his painting. He promised Adam he would not sell it; however, neither would he allow it to be destroyed. It represented his best work and, as an artist, he couldn't let them willfully destroy his masterpiece, whatever their—or Adam's—emotional feelings.

Adam left, conflicted. He loved his uncle; however, already his father needled him about the painting. Accusing him of posing for it as an embarrassment to him. Him! When he wasn't the subject of the painting, Adam was. His father said Adam did it to force his father to up his allowance. Well, his father declared, he would cut his allowance. And so, he had.

Adam strove to hide the truth from his mother. He didn't want to bring her into the arguments with his father. He made it through his university studies with threadbare shirts, worn cuffs, and a loss of weight because of malnutrition, but he made it. His eyes sunk in their sockets. His mother exclaimed at his condition at the end of his studies and forced the truth from him. Angry at her husband, and equally angry with her son, she set about to resolve matters in the only way she knew how, by teaching Adam her financial knowledge.

When the old earl finally died, Adam had gained enough through his investments that he did not need the measly quarterly allowance the earl gave him. But he needed the knowledge his mother shared, and he dove into the reclamation of the family properties with zeal and vengeance.

"Think a moment," his mother said, "and you may come to the same conclusion I have. What do you know about the family Miles is marrying into?"

Adam struggled to shove aside his memories. He shrugged. "They're not particularly political, being more involved in the arts—Are you suggesting that with their ties to the art world they may know where that damned painting is?"

"I am. The Dowager Duchess of Malmsby is known for her art collections and her youngest son runs an exclusive gallery in Mayfair."

Adam struggled with the emotions roiling in his

chest. "You are correct. I need to pack my portman-teau. I need to go to London immediately."

"No, Adam. Not immediately," his mother said, idly, running her fingers through the fringe edging the shawl draped across her lap. "You have guests arriving tomorrow. Remember how helpful their visit could be for the estate. You cannot go running off after just a hint of the painting's whereabouts surfaces. It has been missing for twelve years. It can stay missing a few weeks more. Besides, it will take me time to get ready for a journey to London."

"You want to go to London? You haven't been in years!"

"True. However, Miles is my brother Samuel's son, and he's now a duke, an elevation he neither asked for nor wanted. He needs his family's support. I wish to go to London, and you must escort me."

Adam compressed his lips. He could not naysay his mother. If she thought she should go to London, he would not argue against it, but do all he could to see to her comfort and care.

"And besides," she added impishly. "I would like to see *Adam in the Garden of Eden* again."

Adam felt the flash of cold and heat surge through him again. "The only thing that is going to see that painting is a torch!" he ground out.

CHAPTER 4

RAVENHEART INN

It was late the following day when the Littledean's carriage pulled up before the Ravenheart Inn, an old Tudor building of wattle and mud. The carriage yard was busy with traffic. Helena hadn't realized the village would be a center of travel. She took a firm hold of Dessie when she descended from the carriage and looked around. For a moment, her legs trembled, and she grabbed on to the edge of the carriage door to get her balance.

She felt exhausted and, looking at the pallid exhausted faces of her parents, she thought she must look equally ashen. Perhaps the innkeeper had a room where they might freshen up before someone from Mannion Hall came to fetch them. And maybe a bite to eat as well.

She was pleased to see an ostler run up to assist her father as he descended from the carriage. You could tell a great deal about an establishment by their attention to their customers, or so she had learned on their nine-day trip to Devon from Staffordshire. Some of their accommodations had been quite dreadful in the care of their customers, especially their merchant class customers.

She saw Henry directing the removal of their luggage as she walked with her parents toward the heavy oak and iron inn door that stood open, silently welcoming them.

The innkeeper, a bear of a man who would have been intimidating if not for his genial smile and the sparkle in his eyes, greeted them at the door.

"Welcome, welcome! Be you bay chance the Littledeans coome from Zaffordshire?"

"Wayesh," Mr. Littledean said, leaning on his wife's arm.

"Yes," repeated Helena, to ensure the innkeeper understood.

"Ex'lent. Us were told to 'spect ye. Glad they'll be ta knowed ye arrioved zafe, I'll 'ave word zent up to Mannion 'all directly."

He rubbed his pudgy hands together, then gestured them into the Inn.

"Would you have a room where we might freshen up?" Helena asked.

"Zartainly, miss. And perhaps a mug a ale or Deb'n cider wi' a mite a cheese?" he suggested with a wink.

"That would be appreciated," Helena said with a tired smile.

"This way, then." He paused and turned back to them. "Och, but where be me manners? Name's Ezra Simmons, at yer service," he said. "But come, come."

He directed them to a private parlor at the front of the inn facing the carriage yard. "Ken I zend the bey to take da doog fer a run?"

"Yes, please. Thank you so much," she said.

A few minutes later, a young boy with a merry

smile and tawny hair that stuck wildly out in every direction appeared at the door of the tidy parlor.

"Mi da zaid as how yer wee doog cud use a run."

"Yes, this is Dessie," she told the boy as she handed him her dog's leash. "Do not take her around any carriages," she warned. "She likes to chase moving wheels, and she is stronger than she looks. If you're not paying attention, she could pull you over!"

"Yes, miss. We be fine. I promise." He whipped around to run out the door and nearly ran into Henry carrying a white ceramic pitcher of hot water and some cloths.

Henry jumped back a step, swinging the pitcher up and out of harm's way. "Easy lad!" he said.

"Sorry!" the boy called back as he ran on with Dessie.

"The maid will be up directly with some refreshments," Henry told them as he poured the water into a basin on the battered sideboard just to the side of the wide front window and set out the cloths beside it for them to use. "The head ostler told me it would probably be at least an hour before a carriage comes from the hall. I've arranged for a wagon to take the baggage and myself on ahead. We will be there before you."

"Thank you, Henry," Mrs. Littledean said.

He nodded and left.

"He has impressed me on this trip. He is too good to be a footman," Mrs. Littledean observed as she picked up a cloth and dipped it in the hot water.

"Yes," Helena agreed. "We will need to see what we can do to use his talents." She turned toward her father. "Do you have any ideas?" she asked.

"Wayesh," her father said with a wink and a lopsided smile. "LA-er," he said.

"Later?"

Her father nodded, "Wayesh," he said.

Helena sighed and shook her head ruefully at her father. "You are being secretive."

Her father laughed. "Wayesh!"

She glared at him, which only made him chuckle more.

Two hours later, looking out the front parlor window, Helena saw the Earl of Norwalk's carriage arrive at the Ravenheart Inn.

Helena had grown fidgety, pacing the parlor while waiting for their transportation. Dessie trotted after her.

Her parents had accepted the long delay with an equanimity Helena did not share. They conversed quietly as they waited—or rather, Mrs. Littledean conversed and her husband nodded, grunted, or otherwise showed he followed his spouse's conversation.

A gentleman riding a chestnut horse accompanied the carriage.

Helena watched the ostlers run up to the man, bowing deeply and pulling their forelocks. Was this the earl? She couldn't see him clearly for the mill of people, carriages, and horses around the inn yard. The glimpses she spied suggested a tall, lean gentleman dressed in immaculate riding attire. She saw the man look around as he talked to the ostlers. She stepped away from the window. It would not do for her to be caught spying on him like some grubby street urchin!

She turned toward her parents. "The carriage has arrived," she said. She crossed the room to where their travel wear hung on pegs. She grabbed her brown wool pelisse off its peg. It remained unseasonably chilly for the time of year, so they'd journeyed bundled in their winter clothes.

Helena was looking down, buttoning her pelisse when the innkeeper opened the door to the parlor.

"They be 'ere, milord, all nice and comfy like," he said.

She looked up. The earl's shoulders were wider than they had appeared when she glimpsed him out the window, his features strong. His high-crowned beaver hat shaded his upper face, but he somehow looked familiar. Thirtyish perhaps, she mused. Well set-up.

Dessie ran forward to sniff him as he removed his hat. He bent down to give Dessie a casual pat on her head before he approached her parents. Though pleased by his attention to her dog, it disappointed Helena that he turned away from her so she could not yet see his features.

"Dessie, come here!" she whispered. The little dog trotted over to her.

"I am sorry for the delay in coming to get you," the earl said, his voice low, but without bass rumblings. It had a pleasant sound. "We found a crack in one of the carriage wheels that needed repair. That took some time."

"We have been quite comfortable here, my lord," Helena's mother said as she helped her husband to stand. "I am Mrs. Littledean," she said, curtseying. "This is my husband, Josiah Littledean." She laid a hand on her husband's shoulder.

Mr. Littledean leaned on his cane as he looked up at the earl. "P-lz-ur, mma ord."

Mrs. Littledean smiled at her husband, then turned back to the earl. "He said *Pleasure, my lord.*"

The earl bowed his head slightly. "I think I understood that. The pleasure is mine, sir. I look forward to learning the clay business from you."

Mr. Littledean nodded. "Wayesh," he said.

The man's courtesy to her parents impressed Helena. There was no trace of high-handedness, embarrassment, or awkwardness in his manner. She felt a weight she didn't know she bore rise off her chest. Other than her mother's relations, she had had little in the way of pleasant interactions with either the peerage or gentry.

She walked toward her parents and the earl.

"And here is our daughter, Miss Helena Littledean," her mother said, extending her hand in Helena's direction.

The man turned and dipped his head slightly, further surprising Helena. She curtsied.

When she looked up, Helena found herself looking at guinea gold eyes.

Familiar guinea gold eyes.

It couldn't be!

Her breath caught in her chest. Light-headedness swept over her. She unsteadily touched the table next to her to center her reality. Slowly, her world righted, and she could breathe again.

How was it possible?

The man's unusually bright gold eyes were framed by abundant black lashes and surmounted by equally generous black satyr brows. Her eyes travel across his face to take in the straight, strong nose, the chiseled lips, and the square chin with the shadow of a clef in his jaw.

Before her stood the painting, long hidden in her studio, come to life.

Impossible!

Belatedly, she spoke. "My lord," she squeaked. She cleared her throat. "Excuse me," she said. She rudely grabbed a cup off the table that contained a remaining swallow of cider and drank it down.

"I beg your pardon, my lord," she said as she pulled herself together. "Something stuck in my throat."

"No need to apologize, Miss Littledean," he said, but a puzzled expression shadowed his features for a moment.

Helena looked toward her mother. Mrs. Littledean nodded slightly, signaling she saw the resemblance to Helena's beloved painting as well.

The earl had turned back to her father. "I am ready to take you on to Mannion Hall."

Mr. Littledean nodded. "Sh-ank u."

Helena turned to get her parent's garments, glad to no longer be looking into those mesmerizing eyes that had so often haunted her dreams. She had not considered that any real man could have eyes that vivid gold. He had been a fantasy man to her.

Was he the model for the man in the painting? He had to be! Yet what peer would have himself portrayed as a biblical subject in the nude?

This man was not the youth in the painting. In that youth, a joy of life shone out of his gold eyes like a beacon of light. This man had the same gold eyes, but over time, that beacon light had dimmed. She didn't know when her painting was created, for it was not dated. She wondered at the changes in his life that had caused the dimming light. It saddened her, though she did not know this man.

"Your man has arrived and is working with my staff to see that you are comfortable. They are holding dinner for us," the earl said.

"Then we should hurry!" Mrs. Littledean took her husband's coat from Helena and helped him into it.

The earl stepped forward to hold the other side as she guided one arm into the coat. He stepped back quickly when that was completed to allow her to finish assisting with his coat.

To Helena, his movements appeared natural, not considered. Not what she expected from an earl! She was amazed.

She picked up Dessie as her parents followed the earl out of the inn to the waiting carriage. Helena stopped at the inn door to quietly thank the innkeeper for his care of her family and his son's care of her dog.

The earl waited at the carriage door to hand her up the carriage step. He bowed perfunctorily and closed the door, signaling to his coachman to proceed.

Helena stared after him. He seemed so—so regular. She couldn't think of any other term to describe his calm, even demeanor. Despite his title, he didn't appear to possess the trappings of his rank.

How odd.

He was quite unlike Squire Gentry up the road from them in Fenton, or Baron Welbron, their Staffordshire local magistrate—not that she ever thought much of the magistrate. Those gentlemen and their families were polite enough to exchange pleasantries in a distant manner after church services. Never would they have stepped forward to assist her father with his coat! What manner of man was this earl? And what has been his life's journey?

She watched him mount his horse and set off after the carriage, then he switched sides of the road and she lost sight of him.

❦

ADAM HEAVED a sigh of relief as he mounted his horse, Betony, and followed his carriage to Mannion Hall.

He hadn't meant to accompany the carriage to pick them up; however, when the carriage needed repair, he took that as an omen he needed to be more involved with their guests and their arrival. His mother fretted at the delay, and worried for their comfort. He reminded her the innkeeper of the Ravenheart was a capable man and knew his business, both in relation to travelers and to guests of Mannion Hall.

His mother agreed but admitted she had been looking forward to seeing her old friend. He promised her he would see them safely arrived, so he accompanied his carriage to the inn. It would be full dark before they could make their way back and perhaps it was well that someone accompany them.

He knew from his mother that Mr. Littledean had communication issues since his apoplexy. They were worse than he had imagined. How would they have the kinds of conversations he knew he needed to learn about clay and clay mining from a man who struggled to get his words out?

It did not bode well for his goals for their visit.

However, he would not leap to conclusions as his father often had. Life had a way of offering surprises. That is what his mother often told him. She said that was the secret to her investing success. She studied and waited for the surprises.

He acknowledged the daughter as a surprise. She did not appear the simpering young miss, though she had appeared quite shocked to see him. He did that to people sometimes, his eyes being an unusual color. Still, her reaction appeared stronger than most. He flustered her and he had the feeling she did not fluster easily, for it appeared her reaction took her by surprise.

She was a funny thing, not short, though she somehow gave that impression. She was all angles and sharp features. A smattering of freckles chased across her nose below large, whiskey-colored eyes. Her hair was the most brilliant orange color he'd ever seen anyone's hair, and it appeared to fight taming into style, for a halo of wayward strands waved around her face. Looking at her, he was almost surprised not to see pointed fae ears. She had that look about her. He felt strangely drawn to her.

He wondered her age, for she also had a timeless appearance. He knew she would be younger than he, but this woman was no ingenue. It surprised him that a woman of her age was not wed. She might be engaged, he mused. That stray thought irritated him for a moment. What manner of man would be attracted to this fae appearing woman? An interesting conjecture.

No one would call her beautiful.—But *arresting*? Yes, that was a good word.

He smiled at his own whimsy. She intrigued him.
Why her?
—Why now?

He frowned. Instead of thinking about her, he should wonder how Foster would take to a dog in the house that was smaller than he! Foster tolerated his hunting dogs when they came in; however, they seemed to know their place in the household order— or knew Foster's superior place.

He chuckled at his wayward thoughts as he followed the carriage to Mannion Hall.

CHAPTER 5
THE MEET AND GREET

Helena followed the footman—with a surprising touch of trepidation—to the parlor where they were to meet for dinner. Behind the white double doors was a large room done in gold, brown, and white. The coffered ceiling was painted in mini murals done in multiple panels. A formal room, it appeared to Helena as impersonal. At least the bedroom she had been shown to was a comfortable room—an elegant room done in pinks and rose colors, but comfortable. She thought her orange hair clashed with the decor; however, she mused, since she didn't have to wear the room decor, only sleep there, she could deal with a clashing room.

The earl acknowledged her entrance with a faint nod her way; but otherwise continued to speak with her parents.

He did not display any displeasure with her father's slow speech, or at having to wait for her mother to translate her father's words. She found herself fascinated with him. He was so outside of her experience with society.

She sat on a striped cream and gold sofa and

glanced over at him every so often, studying his face, a face aged probably ten or more years from the youth in the painting. She found she liked the maturity on his features. This man was more interesting in the flesh than in the painting.

She flushed at the thought, for the word "flesh" brought images to mind that she hastily shoved aside. Luckily, the earl and her parents were in conversation and did not notice.

The parlor door opened to admit the Dowager Countess, an elegant woman with hair as dark as her son's but laced with silver. If it weren't for the silver strands, one could have mistaken the woman for the earl's sister, never his mother. Her face appeared free of the march of time, her expression lively.

"Elizabeth!" the countess exclaimed.

"Charlotte!" exclaimed her mother. The two women embraced. Helena's mother grabbed the countess's hands.

"You look wonderful!" enthused Lady Norwalk.

"As do you!" her mother said, her eyes roving over her friend's countenance.

While her mother and Lady Norwalk sat together on the matching sofa across from Helena, still clasping hands as they shared memories, Helena rose and went to stand where her father stood by the earl. She encouraged her father to take a seat.

"You know mama and the countess might as well be alone. They will pay no attention to any of us," Helena said, laughter lightening her typically low, husky voice.

"On-e fued wi draw her at-tenjon."

The earl looked at Helena quizzically.

She nodded. "He said, *Only food will draw her attention*," she told him. "My mother often forgets to eat if she is creating. However, she enjoys food when her mind can be brought to remember it!"

"U to," said her father

"Aha! I think I understood that. He said *You, too.*"

A warm flush climbed her cheeks again.

~

WHEN THE BUTLER ANNOUNCED DINNER, Mr. Littledean was seated to the earl's right. Miss Littledean was seated to his left so she might serve as a translator for her father, but with her proximity, it was hard for Adam to center his conversation on her father. He found he wanted her opinion on the widest range of topics discussed that night. It irked him she didn't contribute. She smiled and listened.

He searched his mind for subjects that might encourage her contribution. He did not think she was shy. He saw she listened avidly and responded appropriately, voicing her opinions and not what she thought he wanted to hear. But she did not start conversational subjects. It was like she was studying him as much as he studied her. He supposed that was only fair.

No simpering coyness, but no demand for attention, either. Or was that as much a ploy as the simpering miss? How old was she, and why was she not married?

Thinking of her marriageable age, he wondered about her cousin, who was to marry his cousin. That would be a safe conversation venue.

"Miss Littledean, what do you think about your cousin marrying my cousin, the Duke of Ellinbourne?"

"I think it is wonderful! In her letters, she says she

is gloriously happy, and I believe her. From what she writes, they appear to have a great deal in common—and he can handle grandmother!"

Adam looked at her quizzically. "Is your grandmother a harridan?"

Mr. Littledean snorted. "Sum sae so. Bu, no."

"Some say so, but no?" Adam asked.

Helena laughed.

"Wayesh. Gou, Gou, ma lo-r," said her father.

"When we were growing up, Ann and I spent time with Grandmother. Especially in summer and on holidays. She was fun to be around! And always up to mischief!"

"Wayesh," agreed Mr. Littledean.

"Ann is like a sister to me," Helena said, smiling, her shoulders relaxing.

"Family is important," Adam told her and her father. "When I discovered Lord Keating was interested in courting my sister, I didn't know what to do as I did not have the funds to endower her. It was embarrassing. But we worked it out," he said. He did not relay that his mother was the one to solve the problem of an adequate dowry. Sometimes the memory that he had to ask his mother for help still chaffed. Angelica's dowry should have been set aside years ago. To discover it did not exist, that it had been spent, infuriated Adam once again that his father could play so loosely with funds that were not his to spend.

"Oh! You have a sister? I didn't know. My mother didn't mention her."

"What? —Oh, yes, my sister Angelica. She is married to Lord Ambrose Keating and abides in Kent, close enough to London to feed her taste for town activities."

"You don't share your sister's enjoyment of the city?" Helena asked.

"I enjoy some of the city's entertainments. What I don't enjoy is the *Ton*. There are places and events of interest in the city. The *Ton* parties are not among those I enjoy."

She laughed. "I have not had a London season—though my grandmother intended on several occasions to sponsor me. Mourning duties plagued both sides of the family, so I don't have the background to understand. I have heard my other cousins bemoan the London social scene. My cousin, Lancelot, particularly complains when he must make his bow, which they force him to do from time to time as he is the heir to the Duke of Malmsby dignities." She laughed. "My dear uncle is a terrible hermit. He prefers books to people. It has become an unwritten acceptance in society that my cousin will act as his father's stand-in—much like Prinny stands as regent for his father. But my uncle is not mad. He is an academic."

Adam laughed. "That can sometimes be almost as bad."

"Yes," she agreed, laughing.

"My uncle is the epitome of the absent-minded academic. As his father's heir, match making mamas and young ladies constantly importune poor Lancelot when all my cousin wants to do is retire to his room and write."

"He's a writer?"

She nodded. "He writes the most atmospheric and scary novels—all under a pseudonym, of course. Not ones to be read late at night!"

"Lancelot's twin sister, Guinevere, is likewise besieged. But her 'vice', as far as the outside world is concerned, is that she plays the violin. She plays the violin along with other stringed instruments. She would rather play in a string quartet at a society event than be a guest at that event. They are a delightfully eccentric pair.

Adam grinned. "They sound like it."

Helena laughed. "I fear my entire family is eccentric. Our passions are consumed by whatever art devours our attention. It is frustrating for anyone who would form a matrimonial bond with us!"

"Your comments intrigue me to ask, Miss Littledean, if I may be so bold, what are the passions that consume your attention?"

"Sculpture," she said, a soft smile transforming her angular features into soft planes.

"Sculpture?" he repeated, studying her face as she spoke. She had an expressive face, alive to all emotions. Not at all like the society debs who practiced social posing.

"Yes," she said, her eyes unfocused, seeing inwardly. "I delight in forms taking shape between my hands," she said, raising her hands as if to cup one piece. "Naturally, I love working with clay, as I have done so practically since birth!"

"What is it about clay that you like?"

"Hmm. The material has a cold, slick feel to it. I love pushing, prodding, and stroking it with my hands into the forms I envision in my head." Her words had a sensual form. She stopped suddenly, blushing. Likely embarrassed for her imagery.

Adam found himself jealous of a ball of clay.

"So, you make wares for Littledean Fine Porcelain?" he asked, his voice hoarse. He took a sip of wine.

"Actually, no, or not much. My mother is the chief designer for the company. I prefer larger pieces and I aspire to go beyond clay to learning stonework, sand casting, and bronze casting."

He didn't understand how it could be; however, this slip of a woman captivated him. No society beauty had ever done that. Now that he'd finally gotten her to open up and talk, he felt he could watch her talk for hours—watch the laughter in her eyes, her ready smile, revel in the huskiness of her voice, and the way her hair glowed like fire in candlelight.

Perhaps he'd just been away from society for too long. It was time for a visit to London, or another social mecca. He'd lost touch with the simple joys of talking to another person.

And he enjoyed talking to Miss Helena Littledean. He enjoyed talking to her a lot.

CHAPTER 6

FOSTER AND DESSIE

A footman was lighting an oil lamp in the entrance hall when Helena came down the stairs the next morning with Dessie on her leash.

"I need to take my dog for a walk," she told the man.

"Yes, miss," he said, hurrying before her to open the door.

"Can you advise on which way to take her?" Helena asked.

"To the right be the stable block, to the left be the house orchard and pasture."

"Thank you. I think we shall go to the left." She looked down at her dog. "Come, Dessie, we've had too many days in a carriage. We need to move and get some fresh air and exercise."

Helena grabbed up a handful of her skirt and ran lightly down the steps and to the left, Dessie bounding beside her. She laughed, and Dessie yipped in response.

"Yes, I agree," she said, feeling breathless. She slowed down. "That felt good," she confided to her dog.

A light fog skimmed the ground. She looked across the property to the gently rolling hills. Fog sat heavier among the hills, softening the dark green.

Ahead of her was a small orchard.

"If I let you off your leash, do you promise to stay near me?" she asked Dessie.

Dessie looked up at her, furiously wagging her little tail. Helena laughed again and bent down to release the leash.

Dessie jumped up and down, her little legs like springs, then ran around in a circle before running off into the orchard. Helena followed her.

She was glad she'd donned her half boots, for the dew on the grass would have had her regular shoes wet and muddy. As it was, the hem of her muslin dress wicked up moisture as she crossed the thick, well scythed grass.

There were a few apple blossoms remaining here and there on the gnarled trees, but the spent, browning petals on the ground spoke to what must have been a beautiful show of blossoms recently. A faint scent of apple blossoms lingered in the air.

Helena smiled as she looked at the old trees with their intricate shapes, the ends of the branches like a dancer's expressive hands. It would be interesting to recreate one of these trees in clay, a delicate and intricate challenge.

Dessie began yipping, her bark high, but not in fear. It was her bark of curiosity, letting Helena know there was something here she should see.

Helena followed the direction of her bark. Dessie was at the base of one of the larger apple trees, running around it and jumping up against it.

Helena laughed. "What is it, girl? What has you so

excited? What have you found?" she asked the frenzied dog.

Dessie turned to look at her panting, her tongue lolling out, then she looked up into the tree again and did a series of sharp yips.

As she drew near, Helena peered up into the branches of the tree. She spied a large orange cat sitting in a low crook of the tree staring down at Dessie as if she were some artifact to be studied. The tip of the cat's tail twitched slowly back and forth.

"Ah," Helena said. She looked down at her dog. "That cat looks bigger than you and this is no doubt his home. You are the interloper. Mind your manners and stop barking."

Dessie's head swiveled back and forth between her and the cat.

"Come away now," Helena directed.

Dessie started to come to her, then stopped and ran back to the tree, jumping up to place her paws on the tree trunk as she looked up at the cat.

"Menace," Helena said. She walked toward her dog to pick her up.

"Leave her be," she heard the earl's deep, resonating voice from behind her.

She turned to see the earl astride a horse behind her. It was the same horse he rode yesterday. She had not heard him approach.

"Foster is not upset or angry," he said.

"Foster?"

"The cat. Foster, this is Miss Littledean, our guest, and this is her dog—what did you say her name was?" He looked back at Helena.

"Dessie."

"Yes," he said, nodding, committing the name to memory. "Dessie." He looked up at the orange cat again. "Foster, this is Dessie, and Dessie is a guest. No teasing."

Helena laughed. "You talk to that cat like I talk to Dessie. You know, some would call us daft."

He shrugged and dismounted. "Animals perceive us more than they understand us. Our tone, and pitch, and body movements convey more than our words. I think words are our vehicle to convey perception."

"That is an interesting idea," Helena said.

"Foster is not a young cat. I've had him for at least thirteen years. He is well acquainted with my foibles."

"He's your cat?"

"Yes, as much as any cat is owned. He was to be a working cat; however, I dare swear I spoiled him too much. He seldom sees to his mouser duties unless one finds its way into my rooms."

"I thought all gentlemen preferred dogs when in the country," Helena said, "as they are good for sport."

He nodded. "I have a pack of dogs as well. They are better behaved than Foster there," he said, pointing his crop at the cat in the tree. "But when a cat adopts a person, the person is taken, and the dogs seem to sense this."

"Do Foster and the dogs get along? There are no fights?"

He looked at Foster and smiled. "No fights. Foster intimidates the dogs."

Helena's brow furrowed as she looked at her dog, still at the base of the tree, looking up at the relaxed orange tabby. "I don't think Dessie knows she is supposed to be intimidated."

The earl laughed. "And I don't think Foster knows quite what Dessie *is*," he drawled.

Helena chuckled. "Dessie is a type of small dog that is bred to go into the mines, only as the runt of the litter she was too small for even that! But she is an opinionated little thing, for all she is so small.".

He nodded. "I've seen similar dogs, but as you say, bigger. We should get back to the house. They will have breakfast laid out by now, and I gathered from what you and your mother translated for me last evening, your father will want to be going out to look at our clay seam soon after breakfast."

They turned and started walking back toward the house, the earl leading his horse by the reins.

"Yes, he has ever been a morning person and was often at the factory before all others."

Helena looked over her shoulder. "Dessie!" she called out. "Breakfast time."

Dessie ran after them and had just reached Helena's side when an orange mass of fur streaked past them. Dessie gave chase around the side of the hall.

"Oh, no!" Helena cried out. "Dessie! Dessie! Come back here!"

The earl touched her arm to hold her back when she would have run after the dog.

"Let her go. Foster can take care of himself."

"Perhaps, but I don't know that Dessie can!" Helena said.

He laughed as she ran after her dog.

When she came around the side of the house, she stopped. Foster had stopped and turned to face Dessie. They were within six feet of each other. To Helena's amazement, neither animal looked agitated. They were curious. They stretched their heads toward each other to get their smell, noses twitching.

Foster slowly walked toward Dessie. Dessie stood still, every muscle quivering and alert to jump to the side and run after Foster. But the cat didn't show any inclination to run. Helena watched as they tentatively touched noses.

Then Dessie jumped and ran around in a circle. Foster watched, then turned to saunter toward the house. Dessie followed, actively running from one side of the cat to the other and back again.

The earl came up beside Helena. "I don't think you need to worry about either of them," the earl said, laughing.

Helena shook her head and laughed as well. "Looks like Foster has sorted it out, as you implied he would. He must be part magician."

"He is unique. I suggest you get your dog now. Foster will go in the house through the kitchen, but I don't think cook would appreciate a dog in her kitchen unless it was a spit dog."

"Oh no, probably not. —Dessie! Come here."

Dessie left off running beside the cat to come back to Helena. She picked her up and put her leash on.

"You can go in the house through that door there," the earl said, pointing to a terrace door. "I've got to return Betony to the stable. I shall see you at breakfast."

"Yes, my lord," Helena said, dipping a slight curtsy. "Thank you for taking the time to speak with me this morning," she said, suddenly shy.

"My pleasure, Miss Littledean," he said, touching the brim of his hat in acknowledgement.

Helena stood for a moment with Dessie in her arms, watching him walk toward the stables. He was an interesting man. A more compassionate man than his initial formal manner portrayed—or perhaps more than he would like others to see, she thought.

She climbed the steps to the terrace and entered the house into the parlor they'd been in the previous evening.

~

"THERE YOU ARE, Helena! And here I was thinking you were still sleeping," her mother said from a dark pink upholstered chair near the fireplace. Lady Norwalk sat in a companion chair set at right angles.

"I took Dessie out for a walk."

"Yes, and I see you wandered across the grass," her mother mused, looking down at Helena's dress hem.

Helena looked down at her dress, now wet and dirty with mud and grass stains. She sighed. "Hopefully, it will come clean. At least I had the forethought to wear my half boots," she said.

"Where did you go?" Lady Norwalk asked.

"We found ourselves in a small orchard and there, Dessie found Foster."

Lady Norwalk laughed. "That must have been interesting. Who won?"

"Oh, there wasn't a fight. I think Dessie just wanted to play, and the cat looked at her like she was a troublesome child. I think they are now friends," Helena mused, her head tilted to the side as she considered their behaviors.

She straightened. "The earl had been out riding and came up to us. He performed introductions, and told Foster we were guests," she said with mock seriousness.

Her mother and Lady Norwalk laughed again. "That sounds like Adam. He has some magnificent hunting dogs, the best horseflesh, and prize Devon cattle and, of all the animals, that cat is his favorite."

"He is unlike any cat I have met," Helena admitted. "Do I have time to change before breakfast?" she asked, pulling at her damp skirts.

"Yes," Lady Norwalk said. "Don't hurry, there will

be food available until luncheon, when more food will
be available. People do not go hungry on this estate,
not with Adam as the earl," she said.

Helena curtsied. "I shall see you at breakfast then,"
she said. She carried Dessie out of the room to the
staircase that led to her assigned room. The comment
the countess made about people not going hungry
with her son as the earl intrigued her. Had people
gone hungry in the past? Another interesting facet
about the earl to consider, she thought as she climbed
the stairs.

HELENA WAS TORN between donning a yellow gown or
a more serviceable dark blue gown. She chose the
dark blue, as she knew it would be more practical for
traipsing around a clay mine. It amused her that she'd
even considered the sunny yellow dress. Who was she
trying to impress? Certainly not the earl!

The earl had differed greatly from the man she
met yesterday. He'd been easier to talk to.

She smiled.

Perhaps that was because they were talking about
animals. He'd been more at ease, treating her like an
equal. She'd enjoyed their conversation. It made her
feel better about their trip to Devon. She found herself
looking forward to speaking with him again.

By the time Helena came back downstairs, she discovered the earl had eaten and left to oversee arrangements for them to visit the new mine and her father
was just finishing up his meal.

He dabbed at his mouth with his napkin bunched
in his left hand. "Wa-at n pa-alr," he said as he
grabbed his cane to help push himself to his feet.

"You'll wait for me in the parlor? I'll meet you there in a few minutes."

"No hh-ry," he said as he slowly walked out of the breakfast parlor.

Helena passed on the ham the footman offered her, choosing only toast to eat. Despite her father saying not to hurry, Helena knew her father was anxious and curious to see the clay on the Norwalk estate. If the clay had the right consistency, and they could get it for the right price, they could look to building their fourth bottle kiln and upping their production, even with the cost of goods rising,

She bit into her toast.

All her life, it had been frustrating that people didn't know how to treat her—as someone of the merchant class or as gentry. As a result, both groups shunned her. She'd been a wallflower at public events and regional balls of either class. Perhaps if she'd been beautiful, a diamond of the first water, she would have been sought after. She was an heiress, she supposed. At least the Firkins saw her as one, but with her value tied to trade and not property, it had no sense of permanence to those whose ancestors had always worshipped the land.

Her grandmother, bless her heart, had tried to bring her into fashion; however, she did not, as they say, *take*. Though in fairness, there had been limited opportunity. She had been taken up with mourning obligations from one or another side of her family.

She sipped her tea.

The man she conversed with that morning was the sort of gentleman she would like to marry, someone who would look directly at her when they conversed. Someone with whom she could carry on a conversation. Someone who would laugh with her. And, she admitted, enjoyed their animals. Perhaps a younger son wouldn't be so stuffy about her heritage and would welcome the opportunity to get into trade if he did not go into the military, join the East India company to seek his fortune, or enter the church, as many were wont to do.

She used to dream about the man in the painting, who he was, what he was like. Would he talk with her? She never would have considered that man to be an earl!

It made her wondered who the man in the painting really was. The man she met yesterday at the Inn and over dinner last night, or the man she talked with that morning who obviously loved his cat! Had he changed over time from the man she saw in the painting to the man she met? The young man in the painting had a more open, approachable expression, yet unmarred by life. That was the thing she loved about the painting. That innocence with strength—it had mesmerized her when she first saw it, as her cousin had known it would.

Perhaps the trip to his nascent mine would clear the matter up.

She took one last sip of tea before she rose to join her father in the front parlor.

CHAPTER 7

THE CLAY MINE

She found her father reading a week-old London paper. He'd sat sideways on the couch and laid it open beside him so he could turn the pages with his good hand. He was figuring out how to do things by himself.

Helena smiled. For a long while after his apoplexy, he'd been depressed. He did not try, but allowed others to care for him completely. It had only been in the past few months that he'd begun to do more and to talk more. And she noted his speech was improving. As she thought about it, it occurred to her his change had started after her mother told them about the potential new clay source. When her mother suggested they travel to Devon, at first he had said no, but after a day, he had agreed. Maybe this is what her father actually needed, to get out and about, to try to do things on his own. While his attack had not diminished his mind, it had diminished his will. It was good to see that will come back.

He looked up at her, folded the paper and grabbed his cane from where it leaned against the sofa and stood up. Helena did not rush over to help him as she typically did at home. Instead, she waited for him.

"Are you ready to go?" she asked.

"Wayesh," he said.

A maid stood at the bottom of the stairs with her pelisse and bonnet. Helena was tying the bonnet's ribbons when the front door opened, and the earl came in.

"Good. You're ready. The carriage is out front," he said stiffly.

Helena frowned, for she noted that the earl of the previous night had returned. His voice lacked any of the warmth or the personality she'd heard in it while they stood together in the orchard.

He led the way to the waiting carriage where a footman stood, ready to assist her father up the step. Helena followed her father and sat down next to him.

As the earl joined them in the carriage, Helena quickly realized that would mean he would have his back to the horses. Peers did not do that! She quickly got up and sat on the facing seat.

"My apologies," she whispered, looking down, embarrassed.

"Apologies for what?" the earl demanded.

Her eyes flew up to his face. "For taking your seat."

He frowned and shook his head, but sat down next to Mr. Littledean.

~

ADAM SIGNALED his coachman to depart. He stared out the coach window, frowning.

What did she mean by apologizing for taking his seat? And why, when she said that, did it flash in his mind as appropriate? It wasn't appropriate. He knew that. A gentleman sits with his back to the horses and a woman and elders sat facing forward.

But he heard his father in his head.

Always insist on the honors of your title.

Those of lower rank were to take the backward facing seats. Rank always sat facing the front. Anyone else, unless invited to sit next to a peer, sat with their backs to the horses.

His father was adamant about securing the proper deference from those below him in society, and so he had drilled into his surviving son.

Why?

His father had also been quick to say why Adam was a disappointment. First, he looked too much like his mother and his mother's side of the family. His older brother, David, was in his father's mind, the epitome of what he thought a man should be. A rake-hell, a gambler, and an altogether obnoxious human being. At least to Adam's mind. He'd died when Adam was still at Oxford, in a stupid duel over a mistress. His father had been inconsolable, but said David met his death as a man should. Sometimes Adam had thought his father would be happy to see him meet his end in the same fashion.

How a man who gambled and whored his way through his days and nights could be revered and considered a role model by his younger brother, Adam didn't understand.

His brother's lifestyle activities held little interest to Adam. He liked puzzles and solving problems more than attending parties and gambling. The Norwalk estate, and bringing it back to profitability, was of more interest to him than the latest ton ball. It was a challenge that he'd embraced. His father had not been a good steward of the Norwalk legacy.

Adam had vowed to turn it around and was suc-
ceeding!

When his brother died, Adam had suddenly found
himself at his father's elbow all the time after a life-
time of being ignored, but he never managed to mea-
sure up to the mythically proportioned David. Less
than a year after David's death, with the Norwalk fortune and estate in shambles, the Earl of Norwalk blew
his brains out. Adam's grief had been for what might
have been, not for what was.

Adam despised his father, but he couldn't seem to
shake his teachings. That knowledge ate at his soul.

He turned his head to look at Miss Littledean. "I
insist you trade places with me," he snapped, reaching
his gloved hand out to pull her up to trade places.

She looked at him with wide eyes but allowed herself to move over to the forward-facing seat.

"Thank you," he said as he sat back down.

Adam noted Mr. Littledean watched them closely,
his eyes alive in his partially paralyzed face. "My father had the old-fashioned belief of aristocratic supe-
riority harking back to the feudal ages. That is not an
attitude I choose to go forward with," he explained.

His tone was formal and polite. Inside, he felt a
mass of nerves electrifying his body. Every time he
turned around, his father's teachings fought to take
over his mind. He could not let that happen! His father lived a petty, self-absorbed existence. He firmly
believed he was superior to anyone else—save
mayhap a King or a Duke—by virtue of his title.
Nothing could be further from the truth, as evidenced
by his repeated investment failures. The thought that
a peer could do no wrong was not a sustainable idea.

~

IT HAD SHOCKED Helena when the earl held out his hand to invite her to trade seats with him, and been equally shocked when that accomplished, he went back to staring out the carriage window, frowning.

She watched him rocking with the movement of the carriage. The young man in the painting had matured into a handsome man, albeit one with visible lines of stress on his face. Those lines lent him a gravity that hadn't been in the painting. She had a wild urge to reach across the space between them and run a hand across his brow to soothe his concerns and to make him smile again as he had earlier in the orchard, and as he smiled in the painting.

He seemed to be two men. The reserved formal earl and the open, enchanting young man in the painting.

Enchanting. What a word to think of. Where had that description come from?

It was what she had seen that morning.

She'd enjoyed their light conversation. She wished she could speak to that man more often, for she had truly been enchanted. And a little in love, in that 'warm feelings' manner that makes the world shine.

He turned toward them. "We are almost at the site. It is across that stream," he said.

Helena looked out the carriage window to see a new bridge ahead. As the carriage rattled over the boards, she saw a beautiful, free-flowing stream edged with overhanging trees and a fruit bramble of some kind. She had no knowledge of trees and shrubs and grasses, or their varieties, but what she saw about her filled her with bliss.

"A half mile or so downstream is the estate mill powered by this stream," the earl said. "I'm afraid there may not be grain enough this year to be milled.

The weather has been too cold and rainy for too long."
He frowned. "I worry for the locals."

Helena nodded. She knew nothing about grain
and milling; however, she could understand how this
would plague a property owner. It had been a chilly,
gloomy spring.

Their worlds were so different, their concerns so
different.

The carriage stopped near a fresh scar in a fold of the
land between rolling hills. They had cut away grasses
revealing the light-colored clay beneath. Two men were
digging into the clay and putting it in barrows, but they
weren't using the proper tools, nor was their digging or-
derly. She nudged her father to look. He nodded.

The earl handed her out of the carriage. Even
through her gloves, she felt her hand tingle in response to his. She quickly pulled her hand out of his
grasp once her foot touched the ground. She turned
back toward the carriage, pleased to see the earl
steady her father as he descended the carriage steps.

Helena tucked her arm around her father's nearly
lifeless arm, and they walked toward the men working. It brought back memories.

"When I was eight or nine," Helena began.

"A-te," her father said.

Helena nodded. "Eight then. Father and I journeyed to Devon to visit the Apple Valley mine." She
turned to look up at the earl who'd stopped beside
them. She laughed. "I traveled dressed as a boy," she
explained.

"Wayesh," her father said, chuckling.

"The Earl of Monteith's clay mine," the earl said. "I
have been thinking I should visit his mine."

"That would be a trip worth taking. The better for

you to see the tools your men should use, and how they approach mining the clay."

The earl looked at her. "Is there something wrong with the tools they are using?"

"Well—" she gave a little apologetic shrug. "They are not the most efficient for the job," she said.

"I can tell by your tone and manner that you are carefully choosing your words. Please, Miss Littledean. Instruct me."

"If I remember correctly," she said slowly, "they had well marked out square pits that were terraced, the lower ones lined with timber. I remember asking why some had timber and others didn't. The man showing us around said it was due to ground water rising that would cause the sides to sink."

"Interesting. I have been thinking about water as a future problem."

"Yes." She cocked her head to the side and closed her eyes as she thought about that trip.

"They also used something like a straight spade, a something iron,"

"Tir-in I-on," said Mr. Littledean.

Helena looked at her father. "Tir-in? Oh! *Thirting Iron!* That's what it was called."

Her father nodded.

She turned back to the earl to explain. "It's a long handled flat spade about this wide," she said, holding her thumb and index finger about four inches apart, "and twice as long. They made vertical cuts in the clay in straight rows, then used this other tool, which was called a lumper—I think, I remember that name as it made me laugh. It undercut the clay so they could make a cube. They then used a curved iron spike to pitch the clay squares they'd cut into a cart. All the

clay squares looked so uniform, and weighed about
thirty pounds."

She turned back to look at the earl's new mine
area and discovered the men had stopped work and
leaned on their tools to listen to her. She blushed.

"Think ye might get tools such as the young miss
says, milord?" one man asked.

"Yes. I'll send Tom to Apple Valley to learn more.
I'm sure our blacksmith can fashion what you need."

Helena removed her gloves and tucked them between the two front buttons of her pelisse. "Might I
have a sample to feel?" she asked.

"It will make your hands filthy!" the earl said.

She laughed again. "Such is the nature of clay! I
need to feel it to judge its quality. At home I touch clay
nearly every day."

The earl looked over at the man who'd asked for
tools. "Bobby, bring Miss Littledean a handful of clay."

"A generous handful, please," Helena said.

The man came up the bank to where they stood.
Helena held out her cupped hands to take the clay
from him. Immediately, she squeezed and stroke the
clay between her hands. She was aware of Adam
watching her work the clay. His intense gaze height-
ened her awareness of him. It made it hard to concen-
trate at first, then she became excited about the silken
feel of the clay.

"Hmmm," she breathed out. "This is nice."

Her father brought up his good hand to touch the
blob of clay she held. His thumb stroked the surface,
then plunged into the clay so he could squeeze it.

"Gou—" he said.

"Yes, it is good," Helena said. She held the clay up
to her nose to smell. It had a clean smell. She liked
that. She tossed the clay ball back into the shallow pit,

then walked over to the barrel of water the men used to lubricate their tools and rinsed her hands off then helped her father rinse off his one hand.

She shook the water off. "Oh, dear, I have forgotten my handkerchief today."

"Here, use mine," the earl said, holding out a clean square of linen.

Helena thanked him as she took it from him and dried her hands and her father's good hand.

"Your nose," the earl said.

"What?" she said.

"You have a bit of clay on your nose," the earl said, his voice thick. He cleared his throat.

"Thank you!" she said, quickly wiping the tip of her nose. "Did I get it off?"

"Yes," he said.

A groom from the estate rode up and jumped off his horse. "My lord! A letter has come for Mr. Littledean that the countess insisted I bring to him directly."

"I'll take it," Helena said. She quickly opened the letter for her father. He motioned for her to read it.

She quickly scanned it and raised a trembling hand to her lips.

"Oh, no!" She turned haunted eyes to face her father.

"Mr. Bickley's dead!"

CHAPTER 8

RETURN TO STAFFORDSHIRE

"Who's Mr. Bickley?" Adam asked.

Miss Littledean's face had drained of color. She looked as if she could fall over at any second. He stepped closer to catch her if she fainted.

She turned wide, stunned eyes in his direction. "He is—or was—," she said with a harsh, mirthless laugh, "Our general manager."

"Was he an old man?"

"No, no. Probably thirty-five or so. The letter is from our local magistrate. He says he was murdered!"

Her father grabbed her arm. "Go 'om," he got out.

"Yes, I agree. We must return home immediately."

He nodded.

"I'll make the immediate arrangements for you," Adam said.

Miss Littledean seemed profoundly shaken up by the news. Was it something more than the loss of a valued employee? Did they, perhaps, have some understanding? That thought clawed at Adam's insides. He helped her and her father back into the carriage and ordered his coachman to drive as quickly as prudent back to Mannion Hall.

Miss Littledean clutched her father's arm. Tears silently coursed down her cheeks. Adam discovered he hated to see her consumed by sorrow.

"Tell me about Mr. Bickley. Was he well liked? Did he have any enemies?" he asked, to pull her out of her ruminations on grief.

"I believe he was well liked. At least everyone at the factory liked him and he had a circle of friends that met at a local pub once a week. He always looked forward to those evenings. He worked hard and long hours, especially since our factory manager, Mr. Richmond, died three months ago. Mr. Richmond had been ill for some time, so Mr. Bickley and I had become accustomed to running the factory ourselves during his illness. We thought he would be better soon, so we didn't hire a replacement. Once he died, we became too busy to think of a new factory manager—though Mr. Stringer has been hinting he would like that position," she told her father.

He nodded.

"He liked the business. More than that, Mr. Bickley *believed* in the business."

"Wayesh," said her father emphatically.

"He was a loyal employee, then?"

Miss Littledean smiled sadly. "Definitely. After father's apoplexy, he was afraid we would sell the business and he might be out of work should that happen; but he was pragmatic enough to know that, as I am father's only child, I stand to inherit the business so ownership changing hands would come one way or another over time."

Mr. Littledean patted his daughter's hand as he nodded.

Adam realized then that the merchant class could

be as shackled to their businesses as the aristocracy was to their estates, with marriage as currency.

Mrs. Littledean and his mother must have been watching for them, for as the carriage drew up before Mannion Hall, the two women came out the front door. Mrs. Littledean ran toward the carriage while the countess waited on the doorstep.

"What is it?" she asked, her fingers tense as she clutched her shawl about her shoulders.

"We must immediately return to Staffordshire. Mr. Bickley is dead," Miss Littledean told her mother as the footman handed her down from the carriage.

"Dead? Mr. Bickley? I knew when the letter came it was bad news, but Mr. Bickley?" Mrs. Littledean exclaimed.

"Yes." Miss Littledean looked at the groomsmen and servants standing nearby. "We'll discuss this inside. I could use a cup of tea."

Adam approved her forbearance with his staff about. He assisted Mr. Littledean from the carriage and the four of them walked to the house. His mother looked inquiringly at them. He shook his head slightly.

Adam directed his butler to serve tea in the drawing room. "And fetch the brandy and glasses from my library," he told him.

"And could you please have our man, Henry, come to the drawing room? There will be much to do to prepare for our departure," Miss Littledean said.

"Yes, miss."

"There is more than just Mr. Bickley is dead, isn't there," said Mrs. Littledean once they were all seated in the drawing room.

Adam watched Miss Littledean inhale deeply before answering, gathering herself, he thought.

"The letter was from Baron Welbron," she turned toward Adam, "our local magistrate," she explained. She looked back at her mother. "Lord Welbron said Mr. Bickley has been murdered."

"What? How? Who?" Mrs. Littledean said.

"The who is unknown. Let me read to you his letter."

She unfolded the paper and paused, staring at it for a moment. Adam thought she was wishing the letter would say something different on this second reading.

Mr. Littledean,

It is with regret that I write to tell you of the demise of the Littledean Fine Porcelain's General Manager, Mr. Charles Bickley.

Mr. Bickley was found on the canal footpath, stabbed to death.

"On the canal footpath? What was he doing out there?" Mrs. Littledean asked.

Miss Littledean shrugged and turned back to the letter.

I have conducted an investigation and can find no one who saw anything or could offer an explanation as to why Mr. Bickley would be at that location. The last anyone saw him was at the Clay Pigeon Pub where he had dinner and socialized with a group of managers in the city. I'm told it was a weekly gathering.

Rest assured, I will continue to be asking questions.

I look forward to speaking with you upon your return to Staffordshire.

Respectfully,

William Augustus Welbron

Baron Welbron

Magistrate

~

THE BUTLER BROUGHT in the brandy and glasses. Henry followed him in.

"Oh, good, Henry," Mrs. Littledean said. "You're here. Please immediately see to the packing of our things. We will leave ..." she looked between her husband and daughter for guidance.

"We need to see about transportation," Miss Littledean said.

"I will make my traveling carriage available to you," Adam said.

"Oh, no, we couldn't take that! You will need it to travel to London for the family wedding!" Miss Littledean protested.

Lady Norwalk laughed. "We have another! I have my own travel carriage. You won't be putting us out to take the estate travel carriage."

"I agree with my mother. And I must admit, her carriage is nicer than mine," Adam said. "And with two coaches, we have two coachmen."

"My coachman is the eldest son of Adam's coachman," the countess explained, still laughing a little. "The late earl and I were estranged for many years, so we came to have two households. I continue to have my own retinue; but with me temporarily living here with Adam, they have become a lazy lot." She looked at Mrs. Littledean. "That's why I said we had plenty of servants here and asked you not to bring yours."

"If you are certain ..." Mrs. Littledean said.

"We insist," Adam said. "You can leave after luncheon if you wish. My coachman will arrange for fresh horses and postillions at each stop. I will confer with him as to how far you might travel today and send word ahead."

He saw Miss Littledean breathe a sigh of relief and her tense features relaxed.

"Thank you, thank you both," Miss Littledean said, smiling, her eyes glistening.

Adam felt good that he could bring a slight smile to her face. He wished he could solve all her problems as easily. He hated to see her go. She was the most fascinating woman he could remember ever meeting. He was looking forward to getting to know her better.

IT WAS a little past one in the afternoon when Helena and her parents boarded the Earl's carriage for their return trip north.

Helena hated having to leave so soon. Less than twenty-four hours! She was not looking forward to more days on the road. Her backside hurt just contemplating the trip. At least with the Earl's carriage and his coachman, they would be more comfortable and make better time. The truth was, an earl's arms on the carriage door would command better horse flesh and service than they'd experienced traveling to Devon.

"You look melancholy, Helena," her mother said as they gently rocked down the road in the well-spring carriage. "Is it more than Mr. Bickley's death that has you so subdued?"

Helena smiled wanly. "I admit I enjoyed conversing with the earl. Neither of us had pretensions of interest in the other so we could relax. I hadn't realized how stultifying the conversations between young ladies and gentleman of marriageable age were, their thoughts swirling around their acceptance of the other person as a suitor or attempts to depress pretensions. With the earl, we just talked. And he listened to me."

"Did you tell him you own his portrait?"

"No!" Helena exclaimed, mortified at the idea. "Besides, what if it is not him, and only someone who looks like him?"

Her mother laughed. "Oh, I assure you, that painting is of the earl. His mother and I discussed it. She is the sister of Clarence Wingate, after all.

"Elizabeth said the summer her eldest niece became engaged, the extended family gathered at Ellinbourne. She said her son and her nephews, Sebastian Redinger and Miles Wingate, liked to swim in the pond on the Ellinbourne estate. They swam nude, as boys often do, and on one occasion their uncle Clarence accompanied them, sketchbook in hand. He drew pictures of all of them, but it was only Adam who he used for his Adam in the Garden of Eden painting. With his name, he claimed he couldn't resist.

"Clarence Wingate displayed the painting to the family when it was completed. Adam's female cousins shrieked in embarrassment and his male cousins teased him unmercifully. And worse, his father laughed at him for posing for the painting, which it is my understanding he didn't actually do. The old earl claimed Adam brought shame to the family by the nude painting." She shrugged a little. "So, you see why the earl hates that painting. His father made his life miserable as he always brought up the painting and how Adam had to have posed for it."

"Young Adam tried to buy it, but his uncle refused. He made his uncle promise that if he ever came to sell the painting, Adam would be who he sold it to. Unfortunately, his uncle did not keep his promise."

"How awful. I wish I had said something. I would

have told him I have the painting and promise I will not sell it!"

Her mother shook her head. "He would not be happy with your promise, not with a similar promise broken before you."

Helena frowned, troubled. She loved that painting. The young man in the painting had become her dream man, both personally as a woman and professionally as an artist. She struggled with the jumble of feelings she had for the painting and for the man. "I suppose," she said reluctantly, "if he felt that strongly about owning the painting, I would give it to him."

"Even if you knew the only reason he wants the painting back is so he can destroy it?"

"No!"

"That is what his mother told me."

"Oh no. He must not know, then. I could not bear for that painting to be destroyed."

"That may not be possible. His mother knows you have the painting as we discussed it just this morning, and how you came to have it. She found the story charming but doubts her son will."

"He'd have to come to Staffordshire to claim it and I doubt he will do that," Helena said.

"Remember, you will see him again at your cousin's wedding."

"Oh, dear."

"Yes, oh dear."

Mr. Littledean, who had been listening to his wife's and daughter's conversation, laughed.

CHAPTER 9
A PRISONER OF THE PAST

Adam paced the drawing room.

His mother sat on the sofa, moving her tatting bobbins over and under and around to create the intricate pattern of the lace trim she would have her dressmaker add to a new dress. Occasionally, she glanced up at him, an amused smile gracing her lips.

Foster sat at her feet, licking a paw, then rubbing his face.

Neither of those occupants appeared the least concerned by Adam's pacing. He had been in the same irritable, grouchy frame of mind for the past four days, though he wouldn't admit it.

"You are concerned for the Littledeans," his mother placidly observed.

"No. . . Yes! Dammit, they've not the wherewithal to handle a murder," he ground out.

"And you do?" she asked.

He ran a hand through his dark hair. "If Mr. Littledean were whole—"

"His mind is not damaged," his mother reminded him.

"Yes, I am aware of that; however, he cannot communicate properly. And because of that, he remains silent, letting others speak."

"True, though I noted he interrupted when he felt it needful."

"A murder investigation demands questions and answers," Adam declared as he paced.

Lady Norwalk laid her bobbins down on the tatting pillow in her lap and set it aside. "And you are wise to the questions needful to investigate murder?"

He had the grace to blush. "All right, I do not; however, asking questions could get one into trouble. I do not wish to see Miss Littledean or her mother stirring up any bees' nest. And they would. Miss Littledean seemed to hold this Mr. Bickley in high regard." He frowned.

"Did that bother you?" his mother asked mildly.

"What? No, of course not. Why should that concern me? That is no concern of mine," he ended harshly.

His mother raised an eyebrow.

"What?"

"It appears it does concern you."

"Feminine nonsense," he said.

Though he thought of Miss Littledean at odd times. She had an expressive countenance that he could not forget. He liked the way emotions played across her face, from laughter to deep thought to everything in between. And those adorable freckles! He remembered how outside, in brief moments of sunshine, the light danced in her sherry-colored eyes. And she always seemed to fight against her independent, flyaway orange hair, little appreciating how it expressed who she was. He'd never seen hair that color before—save on his cat—and he'd wondered what it would be like to set that mass of orange hair free to tumble down her back.

A surprising tightness suddenly inflamed his loins. He stopped pacing, his back to his mother as he willed the sensation to pass.

He grimly shut down his line of thought about Miss Littledean and the emotions that assailed him in its wake. Why her? Why now?

The Littledeans were good people. His father had been wrong to harangue the merchant class, saying they were nothing better than grubby thieves and charlatans.

Class.

And what comprised a class anyways? And what made one better than another? Rank?

His family's title came as a thank you to his great-great-grandfather for services to the crown, not for anything his father or he did, yet that great-great-grandfather's descendants reaped the benefits of his service whether or not they were likewise good people. Rank became hollow with time, a mere salute to the past.

Money?

There were many with high rank and low pockets. He should know as he had struggled with the legacy left to him by his father—plenty of land, but land neither plentiful in production nor rents.

The late Earl of Norwalk had been wrong about much in life. Arrogantly, blindly wrong and those wrongs he taught his sons.

Though now, while Adam might stand aside and see the mistakes his father made, he found it harder to disabuse himself from his father's teachings. They seemed to have seeped into his soul, clasping it with needle-like claws embedded deep.

He did not choose to be the man his father was. He stared up at the white painted coffered ceiling with its angel mural panels. How could he rip out those claws without destroying himself in the process?

"You could go to Staffordshire," his mother suggested.

"What?" His brow furrowed. "Why should I do that? And Tom is not seasoned enough to take on the estate," he said, though the idea teased him.

"Well," his mother said casually. "There is the matter of the painting."

Adam whirled about. *The painting!* "My painting?"

He sat down in the chair at his mother's elbow. "What are you talking about?"

"Adam in the Garden of Eden."

He grabbed her forearm.

She tried to pull her arm free, but he had it in an iron grip. "Adam, you are hurting me."

Adam let go of her arm, jerking his hand back. "My apologies, mother. You shocked me. I over re-acted. What has the painting to do with the Lit-tledeans? What about the painting? What do you know?"

His words tumbled out of his mouth. The painting had caused years of mental anguish. While his cousins' laughter had embarrassed him, it was his fa-ther's harsh, belittling comments that had wounded the most. Adam had not modeled for the painting, and so he had asserted. Even his uncle said the same. He'd drawn sketches of all the cousins that day after they'd removed their clothing and jumped into the stream. Adam had the most mature body of the cousins, and that was the reason Clarence Wingate had chosen him to paint.

His father scoffed and declared Adam had shamed the family by posing.

Lady Norwalk rubbed her abused forearm. "Elizabeth told me your resemblance struck her to the young man in a painting in her home."

"It's displayed?! In Staffordshire?"

Lady Norwalk laughed at the expression of abject horror on Adam's face. "From my understanding, no, it is not displayed. It is actually hidden behind a Holland cover."

"Hidden? It should be more than hidden. You know my feelings on the matter. It should be burned!"

"You are much too sensitive about the painting. Your father was wrong, and you have allowed too many of his beliefs to rule your life. You need to let him and his words go," she said. "You are a strong, capable man, yet concerning your father, you are still a little boy."

"Nonsense."

"Is it?" Challenged his mother. She looked pointedly at him.

He shoved her words aside. "How did you and Mrs. Littledean determined it was the same painting?" he asked, part of him hoping they were mistaken, part of him hoping they weren't.

"I asked her to describe the painting, which she did."

Adam ground his teeth.

"When she said Clarence Wingate signed it, then of course I knew what painting it was."

He leaned forward. "How did she come by it? Why is it in her home?"

"She is not the owner of the painting," his mother carefully clarified.

"Mr. Littledean owns the painting?"

His mother shook her head, holding back laughter. "No. It is in the possession of her daughter, Helena."

"Miss Littledean owns the painting?" Abject embarrassment coursed through Adam. "She never said a word."

"How could she? How could any gently reared young lady say to a man she had just met that she owned a painting of him in the nude?"

Adam laughed harshly. "What gently reared young lady would own such a painting? Such works are generally in the possession of courtesans."

"Well, that does not describe Miss Littledean, so don't even allow that thought to rest a moment in your brain. Miss Littledean is a sculptress, as is her mother. But she is a sculptor of the human form so appreciates paintings of the human form as well as sculptures," she explained. "According to her mother, the painting is an inspiration piece for Helena."

"Inspiration piece?" Adam choked, his voice cracking as his mind swirled with thoughts of the orange haired fae creature seeing him nude as any form of inspiration. He felt the heat rise in his neck again.

He cleared his throat.

"I don't understand. How did Miss Littledean come to own my uncle's painting?"

"Lady Travis had the painting. I don't believe you ever met her. She is Lady Oakley's older sister. Her husband was in diplomatic service, so they were often abroad. Preferred it, I believe."

Adam agitatedly rolled his hand in a circle to urge her to get on with the story.

His mother sighed. "I don't know how she came to have it, if she bought it from my brother directly, or second, third, or fourth hand. Anyway, when her husband died in 1813, she decided to sell the entire art collection they acquired in their years abroad. She wanted to emigrate to the United States, away from all the Napoleon upheaval.

"She was a long-time friend of the Duchess of Malmsby," his mother continued. "She knew the duchess had an extensive art collection and offered her first right of refusal on all the art pieces if she came to Sicily to see them."

"During the height of Napoleon's control of much of the Mediterranean countries?"

"This was when Sicily was a British protectorate."

"Still, to sail past France and into the Mediterranean had to be risky!"

His mother shrugged. "I don't know. All I know is what Elizabeth told me. The duchess took two of her granddaughters, Miss Littledean, and Miss Hallowell with her. Miss Hallowell is, if you recall, your cousin Miles's fiancé. Also, with them was the duchess's daughter, Suzanne, and Suzanne's husband, Lord William Candelstone."

Lady Norwalk frowned. "Lord Candelstone is—or was—I'm a bit unsure of the particulars, a spymaster for the crown."

"E'gads. A spymaster escorted a gaggle of women to the edge of a war zone?"

His mother shrugged slightly. "Elizabeth and I did not discuss Lord Candelstone."

Adam shook his head, but motioned for his mother to continue.

"The painting was to have been shipped to the duchess, but it seems Miss Littledean changed the shipping label to ship it to her home."

"Who knows she has it?"

"Elizabeth told her mother that Helena has it. The

Dowager Duchess of Malmsby has a reputation for being a prankster. It wouldn't surprise me if she hinted as much to your cousin Miles to see where that tidbit of information would go."

"Based on his letter, and its vague suggestion, that sounds as if that is precisely what the duchess did."

"So, you see, you have two-fold cause to go to Staffordshire. First to aid the Littledeans—an Earl's title stands for something, you know."

"Yes, I know," he admitted.

"And second, to negotiate for the painting."

"You don't think Miss Littledean would just give it to me if I asked?"

"No, especially if Miss Littledean were to know you intend to destroy the painting."

Adam had the grace to blush. "I already informed her of my intention to destroy the painting. She looked surprised and horrified. I assumed she was horrified at the destruction of a Clarence Wingate painting, not that she was familiar with the piece."

"What is the harm in allowing her to keep it?"

Adam squirmed. "It is not proper," he finally said.

"Oh, fudge. They hide it behind a Holland cover."

"I remember my cousins' laughter."

His mother inhaled deeply. "You were all young men," she said, sympathetically, "ripe for any opportunity to tease each other."

"It wasn't just my cousins," protested Adam.

"You are thinking of your father's reprehensible behavior."

"How could I not?"

"Your father was mindlessly cruel."

Adam snorted. He rose from the chair and resumed pacing. "Mindlessly cruel? Hardly. Deliberately cruel because he hated me."

"Hated you? No, he hated life. He was a miserable man, so he strove to make everyone around him miserable."

He paused as he looked over his shoulder at her. "He loved David."

"You think so?" his mother scoffed. "Why do you think David became as wild as he did? It wasn't because your father showed him affection and appreciation! He was as cruel to David as he was to you, just in different ways. He found your emotional weak spots and played upon them. Your brother liked mathematics and excelled with them. He may not have resembled my side of the family as you do; however, he inherited a love of numbers from me. That was what your father attacked mercilessly. He wanted David to be a man about town, someone who hired people who were good at numbers, not someone who was good at numbers. And so that is what David became. To please his father," his mother finished with disgust.

She rose from the sofa and walked over to Adam.

He stopped his pacing to look at her.

She put her hand on his shoulder.

"Don't be a prisoner of the past. Make your life your own, free from anything your father ever said or did. I am so proud of what you have done with the estate. Even refusing to accept my offers of money. You have proven your worth over that of ten men. Go help the Littledeans," she said, her eyes misty. "You will feel better for it."

CHAPTER 10

THE MAGISTRATE VISITS

The Littledeans were bleary-eyed and exhausted when they stumbled out of the carriage midafternoon eight days later at Tyche Manor. Helena wondered how the coachman could drive the coach for hours on end, even with postillions riding the lead horse.

She thought she'd forever feel the ground rock beneath her feet. Even at their overnight stops, in her sleep, she felt the carriage sway. She wondered if this was what they meant by sea legs when one took to a ship for an extended voyage from London to India.

Every muscle hurt, including some she wasn't aware she had.

She followed her maid, Eloise, to her room and collapsed on her bed. She would have slept fully clothed if her maid hadn't pushed and prodded her to remove her garments before tucking her under her counterpane.

She gave instructions to Eloise to wake her in two hours. There was work to be done before the day ended. She just couldn't face it without at least an hour of sleep.

When her maid roused her, Helena lay on her bed for a moment to remember where she was and why she was there.

Yes. Mr. Bickley. He was dead, brutally murdered!

She sighed as she stared up at the bed curtains.

He'd been a good man. They'd worked together well in running the factory during the time since her father's apoplexy. What would she do without a general manager? She loved running the company in partnership with Mr. Bickley. What other man would work with a woman and listen to her suggestions with gravity and thoughtfulness? But she admitted to herself, she did not want to run the company day after day for the rest of her life. She wanted a family, and she wanted her art.

They must discover his murderer else all of Littledean Fine Porcelain might be at risk.

Her thoughts settled her resolve. She rose from her bed and looked out the window. Dusk swept across the yard. Soon it would be full dark.

She dressed in a serviceable gray gown without adornment. It was her nod to mourning attire as she did not own black clothes, and though not a relation, she felt she needed to acknowledge the man's demise.

When she came downstairs, she found her mother before her. She said Mr. Wolversham was helping her father to dress and he would be down shortly.

Helena sighed deeply as she acknowledged her mother's words.

"We can expect the magistrate this evening. We sent word to him we have returned and his reply came swiftly. That has an ominous feel to it," her mother said.

"Yes. I'll own I'm not fond of the man. His mind

leaps in unexpected directions. But let's not borrow trouble without knowledge."

Her mother looked at her in surprise. "Since when did you become so wise?"

"Years of listening to you and father," Helena said drily.

The women laughed together.

"I also notified Mr. Drummond of our return. I wouldn't be surprised to see him as well, though he has not responded as such, yet," Mrs. Littledean said.

"Gracious! You have been busy!"

She shrugged. "Unlike you and your father, I can sleep easily in a carriage. I am not in the least tired."

Well, I should be glad that one of us is not," Helena said. "I am rested from my nap; however, my body craves more."

Her mother nodded. "That is how it often is. Cook is putting together a light dinner for us. Since no one was expecting us, there was not much available; however, she promises to have something in an hour."

"I'm going to my studio until then. Send someone to fetch me if the magistrate or Mr. Drummond arrives," Helena requested.

"Going to study a certain painting?" her mother asked archly.

Helena raised an eyebrow as she shook her head. Her lips twisted into a wry smile. "No, I'm going to do some sketching. It relaxes me and opens my mind to think."

Her mother looked at her doubtfully. "All right. I'll send a footman for you, as you suggested."

Helena went down the hall to the back of their stout, red brick manor. It was a portion of the house her mother and father had not spent time nor money on. The rooms tended to be colder and shabby. Helena didn't mind. The old orangery off the back west corner of the house was her sanctuary.

She lit a lantern in the hallway and another in her studio. Shadows were lengthening. Brilliant reds and yellows painted the clouds beyond the many windows of her studio. She stared at them for a moment, drinking in the shades of color and the strength of the shadows.

She took paper and fastened it to her drawing board. With board and pencils in hand, she slowly approached the covered painting.

She stared at the canvas covering. She'd thought the man in the painting to be a fantasy so had previously allowed her mind to daydream, inventing scenarios for who he was, and a history for the painting. To meet the man had shaken her. He was not who or what she'd ever imagined. She set her drawing board aside and pulled off the painting's shroud.

She inhaled deeply, letting her breath out slowly as her eyes took in every part of the painting. No, this young man was not the man she met. This young man had not yet felt the realities of life, had not had the responsibility for a large estate and its people. There was a gravity in the countenance of the man she met. A heavy maturity. Glimpses of the young man in the painting only came to the surface when he talked about his cat.

She smiled to herself as she thought about the earl and his cat. She'd never known a man to be so at ease with a cat. If he were a magical man, his cat would be his familiar.

She picked up her drawing board and began to sketch his face, his head turned in the same manner as the painting. Her sketch showed the same handsome features but layered with the maturity of the man today. You could see it in his eyes, in the thinner set of his lips, the hardness of the jaw, the deeper clef in his chin. Subtle differences.

She wished she could paint. She shrugged. It wasn't where her talent lay.

She could do a bust of him in clay. *Yes.* That idea excited her. She would get to work immediately!

She set her drawing board on the easel in front of the painting and crossed the room to the large wood bin where she had clay stored wrapped in wet cloths. She was relieved to see it had remained pliable. She used a wire wrapped around a piece of wood at either end to cut a piece of clay large enough for the bust she had in mind. She carried to her workbench. She stared at it, seeing the bust in the clay. She brushed a strand of hair away from her eyes with the back of a clay covered hand.

"Helena, it is too dark to work now. Come and eat," said her mother from the doorway.

Helena looked about her. It was dark. How had she not noticed? The lantern only provided a pool of light on her worktable.

"Yes, I guess it is," she said ruefully. She covered her block of clay with wet cloths and wiped her hands on a dry cloth.

Her mother walked further into the room. She picked up the board with the sketch of the Earl of Norwalk.

"From memory! It's very good."

"Not total memory. I had the painting for the basics. I just added the years."

"He's quite handsome, more so now than then," her mother observed. She looked at Helena. "You liked him."

Helena stared at the sketch her mother held. "In

those moments he stopped being an earl, I believe I did," she said wistfully. "But he is very aware of his title and his place in society."

She laughed. "We are worlds apart. Do not get any ideas! You and father are the anomaly. Your marriage is *not* the way of the world."

Her mother set her drawing board back on the easel and hitched her black wool shawl higher on her shoulder. "You are wrong; however, I will not argue with you. Dinner is waiting."

Helena threw the Holland cover over the painting and her sketch, then followed her mother out of the studio.

THE BUTLER ANNOUNCED LORD WELBRON, the magistrate and the vicar, Mr. Drummond, as the Littledeans were settling into the parlor after dinner. They started to rise; however, Lord Welbron insisted they stay seated.

"We have serious matters to discuss. This is not a social visit," the magistrate said grimly. "It is unfortunate that it is two weeks since Mr. Bickley's death and you did not return sooner."

"We were in Devon when we got your note. We could not have returned any sooner," Mrs. Littledean said.

Mr. Littledean nodded.

The magistrate frowned deeply, giving him pronounced jowls. "I regret that I have no news to impart as to the identity of the murderer."

"Before we get into this painful topic, might we at least offer you something to drink? Some brandy or tea, perhaps," Mrs. Littledean asked.

"Thank you, but no. And perhaps you ladies might wish to leave, as I have unpleasant details to relate to Mr. Littledean."

"No, my lord, we will stay. We are my husband's translators," Mrs. Littledean said.

Helena nodded.

He sighed, "If you insist. Mr. Drummond intimated that might be your decision."

Mrs. Littledean smiled at the vicar. "Mr. Drummond has known us for a good many years," she said.

He bent his head in acknowledgement.

"I have been told by all we have spoken to that Mr. Bickley did not have enemies — at least no enemies that any seemed to know."

"We would have to concur with that," Mrs. Littledean said.

"Mr. Bickley took his position and duties seriously," Helena said.

"And how do you come to know this, Miss Littledean?"

"I worked with him at the office almost every day," she said.

He raised an eyebrow.

Helena knew that expression well. She recited her oft repeated script. "I go to the office daily to act as my father's eyes and ears. I relay to him what has happened in the past day and he relays to me how we should see the situation handled. My father may have been robbed of his voice; however, he has not been robbed of his intellect."

"No, no, of course not. I was not trying to imply that," said the magistrate.

Helena straightened her spine and sat up straighter. "Yes, you were. Everyone does. Nothing could be farther from the truth. My father has a stronger knowledge of the goings on at Littledean Fine Porcelain now than he did when he was hale and hearty."

"Wayesh," said Mr. Littledean, nodding.

"Lord Welbron," interrupted Mrs. Littledean, "we arrived back this afternoon from Devon. After we received your letter, we returned with all speed, our host lending us his personal traveling carriage for the journey. We are tired; however, we are anxious to learn more about Mr. Bickley's death. Please proceed, my lord," she said severely, her chin raised to look down her nose at him.

Helena bit her lower lip to repress her smile. It always amused her when her mother projected the duke's daughter. She noticed Mr. Drummond's eyes dancing with mirth and her father's lopsided twisted grin. Poor Lord Welbron. He didn't know who he was dealing with.

"And who were you visiting in Devon?" he asked.

Her mother stared at him for a moment. "If you must know—and I cannot see why you feel you must —we were at Mannion Hall visiting the Earl of Norwalk and his mother, the Dowager Countess of Norwalk," she said repressively.

Lord Welbron stared at her. "Well, well, yes. And I'm sure that may all be verified," he said, his tone patronizing.

Helena thought if her mother's eyes were daggers, the magistrate would be dead.

"Lord Welbron," interrupted Vicar Drummond softly. "You are treading a dangerous path."

The magistrate turned to the vicar. "We must rule out all possible individuals as perpetrators of this crime. For a potter and his family to be visiting aristocracy—to be in such august circles—is suspect, you must admit."

"And why should our visit to an Earl be suspect?" Helena demanded.

The magistrate laughed. He leaned back in his chair, resting his folded hand on his corpulent belly.

"You could have spread it about that you were traveling to Devon. But you weren't smart in that aspect. I've interviewed people. I know you didn't take any servants with you save for a footman. You could have merely traveled a few miles away. No, I believe you set this up to cover up you true plans, to murder Mr. Bickley."

"What?!" Helena rose from her chair.

There were voices in the entrance hall.

"Sh-op!" said Mr. Littledean.

Her mother rose as well. "It is time for you to leave," she said, her chin raised

"Oh, dear," said Mr. Drummond, shaking his head.

The magistrate surged to his feet. "Your story is nothing but lies. A child can create better fabrications. I should arrest you now for the murder of Mr. Charles Bickley!"

CHAPTER 11

THE EARL ARRIVES

"And you should be laughed at," said a familiar voice from the parlor doorway.

Helena spun around. "My Lord!" she said, her voice soft, catching in her throat.

Dessie yipped and ran over to Adam. He obligingly reached down to scratch her ears.

"Who are you?" demanded the magistrate.

"And who are you to ask, other than some obviously officious individual puffed up in his own conceit?" the earl asked, looking him up and down as he sauntered into the room.

"How dare you! Do you know who I am?" demanded the magistrate.

"No; however, if I were to wager a guess, I would say you are a person making a mummery of the magistrate position," the earl drawled.

"This," Helena said, coming between them, "is the—"

"Adam Waterbury," the earl said quickly.

Helena's heart beat faster. "What are you doing here?" she asked softly, turning to him.

"What?" exclaimed the magistrate.

They ignored him.

Adam took both her hands in his. "I have been on horseback for four days. I had hoped to catch you on the road."

"You almost did," Helena said. A tingling sensation coursed through her body. The earl was here, in Staffordshire. In their home!

"We only arrived back this afternoon," she said a little breathlessly.

"You must be exhausted, my—" Mrs. Littledean began.

The earl shook his head at her.

"—friend," she finished looking at him quizzically.

He smiled at her.

"Please sit down," Mrs. Littledean said, smiling back at him.

Mrs. Littledean looked over at their bemused butler, who still stood in the doorway. "Sutton, bring food and ale for our friend from Devon please, and have the best guest chamber readied," she said.

"Yes, madam," he said, bowing

"Yes, madam," he said, bowing out of the room.

Adam sat and stretched out his long legs in front of him. "My mother insisted I come to offer help. I thought her fears were missish nonsense. I see, dear lady, she was wiser than I." He looked at the magistrate. "Why would the Littledeans wish to murder their general manager?"

"They left without servants."

Adam snorted and leaned his head back against the chair. Dessie jumped in his lap. He stroked the dog's head. "That doesn't address why." He closed his eyes. "I have more servants than I have work for them." He raised his head and looked at the magistrate. "My mother requested they not bring additional staff. And if a lack of staff is your strongest argument, then I believe you have no notion who killed Mr. Bickley." He closed his eyes again. "You are brandishing your sword in the dark."

"If it weren't for Mr. Bickley, my husband might have been forced to sell Littledean Fine Porcelain after his apoplexy," Mrs. Littledean said.

"Does someone want to put you in the position of having to sell the company? Have you had offers?" the Earl asked tiredly.

The magistrate looked at him in surprise.

"Best write that question down," Mr. Drummond told the magistrate in a whispered aside.

"Many," Mrs. Littledean said, "but they have all been ridiculously low."

"Our competitors have been circling like buzzards," Helena said.

"Josiah would sell, if the price were right. We've had several discussions about it."

Helena looked at her mother in surprise. She hadn't known they were actively thinking of selling. She didn't know how she felt about that. She didn't want running the factory to be her responsibility; however, neither could she imagine it not being a part of her life.

"Ha! Now I understand why you have not encouraged young Firkins to court Miss Littledean," Mr. Drummond said.

"A suitor?" the earl asked Helena, lifting his head off the back of the chair.

She blushed. "Not a serious one. At least not to me. Besides, he doesn't like little dogs."

"Ah," the earl said, nodding, closing his eyes again as he laid his head back against the chair.

When their butler returned with food and a

pitcher full of ale, Helena was aware of Mr. Drummond pulling the magistrate aside, urgently whispering to him.

She could not fathom the tale Lord Welbron devised whole cloth. How could he imagine her family to be responsible for Mr. Bickley's death just from the knowledge they did not take servants with them?—Though that wasn't strictly true as Henry accompanied them. It made her wonder who told the magistrate they traveled without servants. And why?

She poured ale into a mug and handed it to the tired earl. She studied his face.

Exhaustion robbed his face of color save for the streaks of kicked up road dust. He'd ridden hard to get to them so soon. Why did he do so? Was it just to please his mother?

"When you are finished, I will show you to your room," she said. "I am astounded you rode all the way here. It's over two hundred miles! I am touched by your mother's and your generosity."

"Are you going to the factory tomorrow?" he asked.

She sat on the edge of the chair at right angles to his. "Yes, I must," she said earnestly. "I don't know how they have fared without Mr. Bickley." She shook her head. "And what you don't know," she continued, "is our accountant, Mr. Wallace, is injured. He broke his wrist and is under doctor's orders not to use that hand. We only have a young student of Vicar Drummond—the white-haired gentleman with the magistrate—helping by being our accountant's hands to write invoices, pay bills, and balance the books."

"The factory is short of staff?" he said.

"Yes. We do have two other good employees who will try to pick up the work. Knowing Miss Velois and Mr. Stringer, they will give their best effort, and the other workers respect them. Unfortunately, they cannot sign for the coal shipments we need to fire the bottle ovens. We consume fourteen tons with every firing, and we do three firings per week."

He raised the drink mug half-way to his lips as she spoke, then paused. "That is a lot of coal."

She nodded. "And a great deal of money. It took a long negotiation after my father's apoplexy to convince the bankers and coal merchants to extend credit, as they typically do. They were quite reluctant."

"Without your father to run the factory, I can understand their reluctance. Perhaps that is what my mother meant when she told me an earl's title may benefit you. She would be quick to foresee the financial ramifications of your general manager's death in light of your father's condition."

The earl finished the last of his food. Helena refilled his ale mug.

"This ale will send me instantly to sleep," he said.

"That is a good thing, then," Helena responded.

Across the room, Lord Welbron appeared to be stiffly giving her parents an apology. Her father nodded and walked him to the door. He appeared to be talking forcefully to the man. Helena tried not to laugh. She knew the magistrate did not understand him, but by now the man was too embarrassed to admit his errors. He tried to look attentive, nodding from time to time. From what Helena could overhear, it sounded like her father was lecturing him on the dangers of assumptions.

"Excuse me, my lord," said Mr. Drummond, coming over to where the earl and Helena sat.

The earl set his mug down and stood up.

"I thanked our dear Lord that you arrived when you did. He does work in mysterious ways.," said the

Vicar softly. "I will be leaving now also. I do want you to know the gentleman means well."

The earl raised an eyebrow.

"I know, I know, he was rash. He has been under a great deal of pressure to solve this murder. It occurred on a public canal path, you know. People are worried we have a deranged killer in our village, as no one can come up with a reason why anyone would want to harm Mr. Bickley. He was well liked."

"So, I have been told. Tell me, how did he die? I know he was stabbed, but little else."

"That was all Welbron said in his letter to father," Helena said.

The vicar nodded. "I asked the physician, as I attended to Mr. Bickley's burial in the churchyard. Dr. Baylor said someone stabbed once him in his neck with what appeared to be a thin-bladed knife. If he had been stabbed any other place, he might have lived; but the doctor said the murderer caught the big artery with his knife and then pushed Mr. Bickley down the canal embankment where he ultimately bled out. He did not land in the canal, which the murderer undoubtedly hoped he would do, so his body might float away from the area before he was discovered."

"Thank you," the earl said.

The vicar bowed. "I shall take my leave now so you may get some well-deserved rest."

Helena rose from her chair. "Good night, Vicar. I am sure we will see you tomorrow."

He nodded wearily and left.

"Now, my lord, I will show you to your room."

~

IT SURPRISED Adam to discover he remained upright. Every part of his body ached. Bed would be welcome. He needed to sort out why he pushed himself so hard to get to Staffordshire. He was certain his mother had not meant for him to push himself to that extent. All he knew is he wanted to see Helena again. He wanted to understand why she seemed so different from all the other women he'd met. She didn't posture or put on any airs. Her conversation was natural. He felt he could talk to her about anything.

He also didn't understand why she would be the person to have his painting over all others. It intrigued him that she liked it. Everyone in his family who had ever seen it had used it as a vehicle for teasing and ridicule. His father had belittled him enough growing up that his confidence suffered for many years as a result of his father's attitude. As an adult, he knew it was jealousy on his father's part that caused the man's meanness. Still, knowing and having the ability to shrug it aside were two different emotions.

He glanced at the woman who walked beside him to the broad staircase leading to the first floor. Her wild orange hair curled around her head and face like a halo. When they passed a wall sconce, it glowed golden in the light.

"You know, don't you," she whispered as they climbed the stairs. Her voice had the gentle, musical quality of sunshine. It warmed him.

Adam saw no reason to play games or otherwise prevaricate. "Yes," he said simply.

She nodded. "Mother and the countess discussed it—the painting," she said.

"Yes, I know. They agreed we should know and decide between us how to handle the matter of the painting."

"I know you want to destroy it," Helena said, looking up at him. "I—I can't let that happen." She turned her head back to look up the stairs. "I couldn't let that happen," she whispered.

"I don't understand."

"No, I know you don't." She laughed harshly, "I don't know that I do either, at least not clearly." Her eyes narrowed as she thought about the conundrum. "It's like," she began slowly, "it's like when I do a sculpture from a lump of clay. I know the shape I want is within that lump of clay, but I can't see it for the raw block of raw material in the middle of my worktable. I need to tease the form forth. So, I need to tease my feelings forth so I might study them."

He considered her words. "You know, I think that is how I am about the painting. I have many memories tied into it, terrible memories, memories I would like to dismiss."

"Destroying the painting will not destroy the memories."

"Perhaps not; however, it would heal part of what is broken."

"What's broken?"

He looked at her sideways, one side of his lips curled upward. "I believe we are alike."

"What do you mean?"

"That is what I'm trying to figure out, too."

Helena stopped by a room at the head of the stairs. She laughed slightly. "We are a pair, aren't we? Both bound up by a painting. Here's your room, my lord."

"You know, I have the strangest desire to hear you call me by my first name." He tucked a strand of her wild orange hair back behind her ear and fought against the desire to allow his fingertips to trail down the side of her neck.

She smiled wistfully. "I have spoken to the man in the painting as Adam for so long, sometimes, when I address you, I have to pause for a moment as I remember *not* to call you Adam!"

He smiled. "As you said, we are a pair." His smile dimmed, his mind racing as he considered that statement. "Do you think we could be more?" he asked, striving for lightness in his voice

"More?" Helena repeated. "I—I don't know." She stared at him, her breath coming faster. He leaned forward to kiss her. She stepped back. "Breakfast is at eight. I'll send Henry up to attend you," she said hurriedly. "Good night, my lord. Sleep well." She curtsied and turned to flee down the hall.

CHAPTER 12

A FAKE BETROTHAL

Adam slept deeply during the night and found on rising the next morning that he had shed much of the bone deep weariness he'd felt the day before.

His body yet ached from long hours in the saddle; however, he felt that would pass once he walked a bit. He was eager to see Helena again. He had ideas regarding investigating Mr. Bickley's murder that he wanted to share. And he needed to see if her reactions to him last evening were true, or the aberrations of a tired mind.

Mr. Littledean was before him in the breakfast parlor, his man, Henry, seated with him. That surprised Adam, but then, he thought, why not if they had business to discuss? Why not over breakfast?

Henry rose when he saw him. Adam waved at him to resume his seat.

"I've had an idea for when I visit the pottery today. I should like to be introduced as Adam Waterbury, not the Earl of Norwalk. You can say I am the Earl of Norwalk's man of business and that wouldn't be wrong, for I am my man of business."

Mr. Littledean laughed from deep in his chest as

he nodded. "Gou, gou," he said. He pointed to Henry. "Shrek-ry."

"He said *Secretary*, my lord. Mr. Littledean has made me an offer to be his secretary."

"Congratulations! That sounds excellent. I suppose your first assignment will be to hire a new footman to replace you."

He grinned. "Yes, sir."

"Mr. Littledean," Adam said. "Can you instruct your staff not to mention you have an earl visiting? Just tell them I came to continue the discussions for the clay purchase but I am now helping to discover who killed Mr. Bickley and we believe people will be more willing to talk to me if I'm not introduced as a peer."

Mr. Littledean frowned a little as he considered the request.

"Mr. Waterbury is right," Henry said.

Adam laughed. "Good man!" He glanced down at his hand, then removed the prominent signet ring of the Earls of Norwalk. He tucked the ring into his waistcoat pocket. "I should start as I mean to go on. So, what do you say, Mr. Littledean?"

His host nodded. "Wayesh, he said.

He turned to Henry. "Te hmm I guo to fak-ry."

"He says to tell you he is going to the factory today."

"And as his secretary, you can speak to the bankers and coal mill owners for him."

"Wayesh," said Mr. Littledean.

"It might serve. You know your daughter is concerned about payments."

Mr. Littledean shrugged his good shoulder. "Wwe-ate oon futh of-n."

"We wait on building the fourth oven, is what he means."

Mr. Littledean nodded.

"Henry, what is your last name? If I am Mr. Waterbury, what do I call you?" Adam asked.

"Franklin. Henry Franklin," he told the earl.

"Mr. Littledean, Mr. Franklin, I should very much like to accompany you to the factory today."

Mr. Littledean nodded, then looked at the porcelain mantle clock, squinting his eyes a bit to see it. "The-T minutes?"

"Thirty minutes?" Adam said before Henry could translate."

"Very good My—Mr. Waterbury," Henry said, correcting himself.

Adam grinned at him and nodded.

"Wayesh," Mr. Littledean said.

"Then, if you don't mind, I will take a walk around your property until it is time to leave. I need to walk after so many days riding."

"Curs," Mr. Littledean said, nodding.

"We'll send someone to find you when his valet, Mr. Wolversham, and I have Mr. Littledean ready to leave."

"Thank you. That would be most helpful," Adam said. He pushed his chair back from the table and stood up. "I'll keep in sight of the house to make it easier to find me," he said.

Adam walked out of the breakfast parlor with a lightness in his step as he considered the possibility Miss Littledean might walk her little dog outside at this hour.

❧

ADAM TROTTED down the five steps from the front door to the drive that curved around the front of the red brick manor house. Last evening he'd ridden up at near dark, so he didn't get a good view of the house. He walked down the drive and turned to look back. It was a neat Georgian mansion, not at all like the rambling hall he'd grown up in. The stables were to the left. He walked in that direction to see to his horse. He'd pushed himself and Betony hard to get there as soon as possible. He had to make sure the mare had suffered no ill effects from the hard ride.

He considered his quixotic decision to go by Adam Waterbury. His father would turn in his grave, his displeasure with his heir multiplying.

Adam's lip curled. Too bad.

He'd known for years that he displeased his father. Even though he knew he wouldn't change the old earl's mind, he'd tried to please him. He didn't know why he persisted though his father was dead— whether that persistence was determination to win acceptance even though he knew that was not to occur, or whether his persistence was spurred by guilt for not measuring up to expectations. He rather thought it was some twisted form of guilt.

He'd had a lot of time to think on the ride to Staffordshire. He realized he didn't owe his father any guilt. Perhaps it was his father who bore the guilt for his stubbornness. Rather than embrace his wife's talents, he'd pushed her away, holding tight to the notion of women as inferior creatures.

What a sad waste. They could have been a leading *ton* couple. His father, for all his faults, had been a creative thinker. If he'd coupled his creativity which his wife's financial acumen, they would have had people clamoring for friendship.

He stopped at the broad doorway to the stables to allow his eyes to adjust to the dimmer light. Just as his eyesight adjusted, he heard Dessie's excited yipping.

"Dessie, what is it?" Helena asked. She turned away from Betony, carrot in hand. "Oh! My lord, I didn't realize you were there," she said, dipping into a slight curtsey.

Betony chuffed and nudged her arm for the treat.

Helena swung the carrot back around to where his horse could grab it.

Adam laughed and walked up to rub Betony's nose as she munched on the treat. "She's a good horse," he said to Helena. "She deserves something delicious after what I put her through the past five days."

Helena nodded, a slight blush on her cheeks.

"I have a request to make. It is one I've already discussed with your father."

"Yes?"

"For the rest of my visit, please don't address me as my lord, or introduce me as the Earl of Norwalk," he said. "I am Adam Waterbury. While we are about in the village and surrounding area, I am the Earl's man of business. As I told your father at breakfast, that is not a lie. I *am* my man of business and Adam Waterbury is my name."

Her brows scrunched together in doubt. "I may do that, but can you?"

"What do you mean?" he asked.

"Leave off the habits of rank and know how to address others? To give deference to the old? To bow and not wait to be bowed to? To not depress pretensions with a withering glance?"

"Withering glance?" he asked doubtfully.

"Yes, that ability to make someone want to shrink to the size of Dessie."

He frowned, then his expression cleared as he considered her words. "My first reaction to your comment is to laugh and deny it. However, on the ride to Staffordshire, I owned to the habits instilled by my father. That was not a happy realization. I will strive for a touch of humility. Do you really think it will be that hard?" he asked, exasperated.

"Excuse me, miss," said a groom at the stable door.

"Yes, Derek?"

"Mr. Firkins and young Mr. Firkins have just arrived," he told her.

"At this hour?"

"Yes, miss."

Her eyes narrowed, then she looked up at Adams. "You are about to have your first test and I warn you; it will be a test. Dessie! Come!"

The little dog popped out of a mound of hay

"You are a mess! Well, come on. You will be my excuse to go in the back way," she said.

"I shall accompany you," he said."

She nodded and led him out of the stable.

"Who are the Firkins?" he asked as they walked toward the back of the house.

"Mr. Firkins own Firkins Pottery, a friendly competitor, one could say. He has wanted to acquire Littledean Fine Porcelain from my father for several years, but he doesn't want to pay a fair price. His plan is to have his son marry me and have a share of the pottery as my dowry."

Adam felt a surge of jealousy. "And what do you think of this plan?" he asked levelly.

"Not much. However, as Mr. Drummond pointed out to us before we left for Devon, I haven't much in the way of choices."

Adam stopped mid-stride.

Helena stopped as well and turned to look back at him.

"What the bloody hell kind of statement is that?" Adam's brows drew together, pulling his eyebrows up like demon wings at their outer corners. "Excuse my language; however, I find that insulting, coming from a man of the cloth."

"I am not a young debutante. I have the most obnoxious orange hair, awful freckles, I am too skinny, and I don't know how to simper.

"Nonsense. Bloody nonsense," he returned fiercely.

Helena felt a giddy shiver run through her at his words.

They entered through the scullery at the back of the house and walked through the butlery. From the hallway to the front entry, they could hear Mr. Firkins thump his cane on the floor in rapid agitation.

"What do you mean it is not your decision who your daughter weds? She's your daughter. She will do as you say. And you know, Josiah, their match has advantages for both families."

"Wayesh," Mr. Littledean conceded, nodding slowly. "Bot Henna nos er on mine."

"What did he say?"

"He said *Helena knows her own mind.*"

"Bah," Firkins said with a toss of his hand. "You're a fool, Littledean. These women ride roughshod over you."

Josiah Littledean shook his head.

"Listen to my offer," Firkins the elder said.

Mr. Littledean saw Helena and Adam in the hall. He shook his head slightly to warn them back.

"Stu-e," he said.

"He asks that you join him in his study," Henry said.

"That's better," said Mr. Firkins, smirking. He followed Mr. Littledean's shambling gait into the study.

When the connecting door from the parlor to the study closed behind the four gentlemen, Helena ran toward her mother.

"What is going on?"

"Because of Mr. Bickley's death, Mr. Firkins believes you should marry his son with all haste, so Tibault can take over the factory for us. He's come to discuss settlements."

"He means so he can take over the business. I said before we left for Devon, I will not marry Tibault."

"I know dear; however, your father worries for the factory and the people he employs."

Helena looked stricken. She turned toward Adam, her color drained, her breath coming faster.

Adam looked at the mantel clock. "He's too late," he said slowly. His mind swirling at the idea that just came to him. He knew how to reprieve Helena and give the Littledeans more time. He turned to look back at them.

"Too late?" Helena repeated, confused.

"Yes." He reached for her hands. "We shall tell Mr. Firkins that not fifteen minutes ago you agreed to my offer of marriage," he said earnestly.

She pulled her hands back. "What? Lie?"

Her mother clapped her hands together and laughed. "That should infuriate Mr. Firkins."

"Though the magistrate and the vicar know the truth, we are to put it out that I am the earl's man of business."

"Yes," Mrs. Littledean said. "And we shall admit

you met through correspondence and spent time together in Devon."

Adam nodded at Mrs. Littledean. "Very good, madam."

"And when we had to leave suddenly you became despondent."

He frowned at this suggestion. "Certainly, I am not such a poor fellow," he protested.

"I beg to differ with you. In this instance you are. So romantic."

"Mother!" Helena fussed.

"I see your point," Adam conceded, thoughtfully.

"You are both mad!" Helena declared. She sat down on one of the facing sofas. "Father will not agree with this."

"Yes, he will if I am the one to make the announcement. He knows I am my mother's daughter," her mother said, laughing. "You can determine later that you will not suit," she said airily. "I find I am quite put out by Mr. Firkins' assumptions. The gentleman is due for a comeuppance. I believe you are correct, Helena, on Firkins instructing his son on all aspects of the marriage bed."

"Mother!—Please!" Helena said, her eyes wide, a heated flush flooding her cheeks, traveling down her neck to disappear under the neckline of her dress.

"What's this?" Adam asked, viewing the deep blush with curiosity as to where it went.

"Nothing, just a brief comment I made *privately* to my mother," she said, glaring at that parent.

Adam shook his head. "Oh, the flights my imagination will take on this subject," he said. "Perhaps Miss Littledean said this...or she said that..."

Her mother laughed.

"Where is a port bottle when one needs one?" Helena said.

"Now Miss Littledean, it is far too early for a lady to be drinking port."

"Who said anything about drinking it?" she said waspishly, raising her arm to mimic brandishing a bottle by its neck.

Mrs. Littledean and Adam laughed again, then Mrs. Littledean grew serious. "If you are to get Mr. Firkins to believe that your arrangement is real, your feelings sincere, you had best begin addressing each other by your given names."

A corner of Adam's mouth wryly kicked up. "That shall not be hard for me. During that tedious long ride, I addressed you as Helena in my thoughts," Adam told Helena.

Helena blinked. "While I confess, I have *not* been thinking of you as Adam. To do so recalls to mind a certain painting."

Adam scowled.

"There see, now if I were to address you as Adam, you will also think of that painting! Do you have a middle name, or some pet name from your childhood?"

Adam thought for a moment, then laughed. "Nothing I would wish to own to. My brother called me Goldie."

"Goldie?—Oh, because of your eye color. No, I don't think I could call you Goldie. That sounds like what I might name my pet."

"What about referring to him as Waterbury?" Mrs. Littledean suggested. "Many men are addressed as their surname."

Helena considered that name. "Yes, that would work."

She stood as the door connecting to the study opened.

"Consider, Josiah, your daughter is not likely to get an offer as good as from my son Tibault, here," Mr. Firkins said, his head turned back to address his host.

"She already has," said Mrs. Littledean said archly. Though seated on the sofa, she managed to give the impression of looking down her nose at Mr. Firkins.

"And I will have you know, sir, I find your comments about my daughter in poor taste."

Adam's mouth quirked sideways in admiration and humor.

Mr. Firkins scowled. "What manner of nonsense is this?" he demanded.

"It is not nonsense," Mrs. Littledean returned. She casually twitched a fold in her skirts to smooth a wrinkle. She looked up. "Helena has accepted an offer from Mr. Waterbury not thirty minutes ago."

"Josiah!" Mr. Firkins roared.

"Wah—" returned Mr. Littledean. He made his way across the room to sit at his wife's side.

"Stop this idiocy!"

"I do—n see id—cy."

"What?" Firkins roared.

"It is simply a matter of listening," Adam said before Henry or Mrs. Littledean could respond. "He said he doesn't see any idiocy."

"Wayesh," Mr. Littledean said, nodding, the mobile side of his face pulling upward and his eyes sparkling.

"No-o-o!" cried out young Tibault Firkins. He crossed the room and slid to his knees before Helena, grasping for her hands, "Miss Littledean, Helena! I always thought we should marry, since we were children!"

Helena squirmed her hands free from his grasped. She stepped away from him.

Adam put his arm around her to draw her closer.

"No Tibault. Yes, we were friends as children, but we are not children anymore and we don't see our way in the world in the same way," she said gently.

"He is not from these parts. How do you know him?"

"We have been in communication for a while, regarding our buying clay from the estate of the Earl of Norwalk and got to know each other through letters."

"Ah-ha!" Mr. Firkins crowed. "The new ball clay mine! How did you hear of it before me?" demanded Mr. Firkins.

"I hv ma sauses," Mr. Littledean said proudly.

"What?" demanded Mr. Firkins, looking about the room.

"He says he has his sources," Henry crisply translated.

"Well, little good it will do you. I've written directly to the Earl and offered a generous price as I've heard his estate is foundering. You'll not be able to offer better than me for that clay."

"Your information is dated," Adam told Firkins.

"Nonsense. And who are you, anyway," demanded Mr. Firkins, thumping his cane on the floor again.

"The only thing that matters right now is I am Miss Littledean's affianced. Sir, I am Adam Waterbury. I am closely involved with the Earl of Norwalk's estate."

Mr. Firkins sneered and looked him up and down. "How so?"

"In many capacities; however, regarding the condition of the estate, I do the earl's bookkeeping. I know precisely his situation. The clay mine is important to the future of the estate. That is true. However, it takes capital to get a mining enterprise started. He has the capital."

"You're a bookkeeper!" Mr. Firkins exclaimed.

Adam nodded. "Among other things, I have had training in that, yes." Out of the corner of his eye, he saw Helena choke back a laugh.

Mr. Firkins turned to Mr. Littledean. "You're allowing your daughter to throw herself away on a bookkeeper? I was willing to believe that your apoplexy did not affect your mind. Now I am not so sure."

Helena gasped.

"That is enough, Mr. Firkins," said Mrs. Littledean, rising to her feet, anger flared red on her cheeks. "You have said quite enough. I shall call Sutton to escort you out." She ran the bell by her side.

"You are all mad!" proclaimed Mr. Firkins. "You'll be sorry when you can't get credit to pay for coal!"

Adam scowled and stepped forward. "Is that a threat, Mr. Firkins?" he asked softly, but with a warning menace in his tone.

"Take it as you will," sneered Firkins. His head swiveled to glare at each of them. He sniffed, then stomped toward the hall. "Tibault! Come!" he yelled.

Tibault gathered his things, including his portfolio, and hurried after his father.

"That's how I call my dog," Helena said.

~

"I NE-D WRI LE-ER TA BA-NK-RS," Henry said.

"Yes," Mrs. Littledean agreed. "I think you should write your bankers now, before Mr. Firkins says anything."

"Do you think he would go out to make mischief right away?" Helena asked her mother.

"Yes, I do. Mr. Firkins is one of those gentlemen who can be a good friend or the worst enemy, depending on what suits his need at the moment."

"Wayesh," her father nodded.

"Henry, while Josiah and I work on these letters, please see about procuring another carriage to take you, Mr. Littledean, and Mr. Waterbury," she said, smiling at him as she deliberately used his family name, "to the factory while Helena and I visit Mr. Drummond and inform him of this morning's activities. We'll join you at the factory afterward."

Mr. Littledean nodded.

They left Helena and Adam staring at each other as the others hurried off to their tasks.

Helena bashfully cleared her throat. "I appreciate this ruse you have partaken in for my family's benefit."

"As much as I like your parents, they had nothing to do with my decision to propose the betrothal," Adam said softly. He led her to the sofa and sat down next to her. He clasped one of her hands in his and rubbed his thumb across the top of her hand.

She tried to sit straighter and pull her hand away, yet he held it fast.

"This is ridiculous!" she said. "It will be most awkward to cry off from marriage once we sort everything out."

"It occurred to me, as soon as it sprang to my lips, that it isn't a bad idea."

She looked up and stared into his startlingly gold eyes.

"When my brother died, and I became my father's heir," he said, "people treated me differently. Suddenly I was a gentleman women wanted to talk to. We were not rich, that was well known as the estate is heavily encumbered. But I suddenly had a Viscount's title and would be an earl. Heiresses courted me for my title, not me courting them for their fortune. My father continually told me that was my appeal to women. There certainly wasn't anything else in me he could see that would entice a woman."

"What?" Helena protested.

"I was not a sportsman like my brother, offering a ready smile and quick wit. My father took great stock in gentlemanly pursuits like sports, cards, and women. He thought my brother was the epitome of a gentleman of leisure. My mother tells me my brother was miserable in the role he had to play, so he played it to the hilt, he played it to the death. And you know something? My father was proud of him for how he died, in an illegal duel."

"Oh, no!" She grabbed his hand, squeezing tight.

"You are the first woman I have felt truly comfortable just talking to," he said. "Let's play this out and see what happens. Right now, I am happy with the idea of you as my countess, but I want you to be happy, too."

"I have been delighted with how easy we can talk together. A bit in awe, too. But I need to time think.

"I know. I, too," Adam told her. "I, too."

CHAPTER 13
UPHEAVAL AT THE POTTERY

Upheaval At The Pottery

By the time the gentlemen left Tyche Hall for the Littledean pottery factory, it was nearly noon. They'd seen the women off to Reverend Drummond, then requested Derek to drive them to the factory. In the distance, Adam noted smokestacks billowing black smoke into a dark cloud spreading across the town.

Mr. Littledean grunted. "Fi-kens and M-feel Pa-ry," he said.

Adam looked at Henry Franklin,

"I believe what Mr. Littledean is saying is the Firkins and Medfield Potteries have bottle ovens firing today."

"Wayesh," said Mr. Littledean, nodding.

As they drove up a small rise, Adam could see the town teeming with activity. Women carrying over-flowing baskets, men in rough clothing, carters, men and boys riding or leading scruffy draft horses.

"Mok-et Day," Mr. Littledean said.

"Market Day?" Adam asked.

His host nodded. "Wayesh."

It forced Derek to slow down to pick their way through the traffic. A few people recognized Mr. Littledean in the carriage and called out to him, delighted to see him.

"You are popular," Adam observed to Mr. Littledean.

Mr. Littledean gave his lopsided grin. He nodded, his eyes alight with pleasure for the recognition.

"You haven't been to town since your apoplexy?" Adam asked.

Mr. Littledean shook his head.

When the carriage drew up before the office entrance of the large brick factory, a man in a leather apron who stood at the courtyard entrance smoking a pipe stared in surprise, then swung around to run into the courtyard. As Adam and Henry Franklin helped Mr. Littledean descend from the carriage, they could hear the man call out to peers, "Mr. Littledean! Mr. Littledean is here!" and then heard other voices taking up the cry, passing the news to others.

Before they could cross to the office door, a swarm of people appeared from within the courtyard. Cries of *"Mr. Littledean! Mr. Littledean, sir!"* and *"Welcome, sir!"* could be heard from the small growing crowd.

The group cheered as Henry opened the office front door and escorted Mr. Littledean inside.

Adam saw Mr. Littledean pull a handkerchief from his pocket and dab at the corners of his eyes. He saw Adam looking at him. "A-waa ta lo-ng," he said. "Foo."

Adam smiled and patted his shoulder. "You're not a fool, sir. And you may have been away a long time, but it looks like you're in the right place now."

Mr. Littledean looked up at him, his eyes glistening. "Wayesh," he said strongly. "Wayesh."

He looked about the room then walked over to a man and a boy standing by the tall desks. He clapped the man's shoulder. "Mer Wal-us." He looked at the boy. "Mer Smi-h?" he asked.

The boy stood straighter. "Walton Smythe, sir."

Mr. Littledean nodded. "Gou la—." He looked about the office. He looked about the office and his bon homme faded.

Adam followed the direction of his gaze.

The office appeared disorganized. Account books lay open on every surface. Ink splatters, much like had happened to Tom at his estate office, but here, nothing had been cleaned up. Correspondence lay in disorganized piles. The rubbish bin overflowed.

"Mer Wal-us!" Mr. Littledean waved his good hand about to take in the entire room. "Wha-s hiss?"

"We— we've been busy, sir. Everything happening with Mr. Bickley and all. Creditors hounding me for payment, the bank not releasing funds, I-I don't know what to do!" the man cried, his good hand pushing what strands of hair he had on the top of his head back in a nervous gesture.

"I un-sta," Mr. Littledean said, his eyes narrowed as he studied the room again. "Hun-ee, fe-h Mer Sho-knd," he said.

"Fetch Mr. Shiskind? The banker?" Henry clarified.

"Wayesh."

"Yes, sir, right away, sir," Henry said, suddenly grinning.

"Mer Wa-bur, I sho- u a-rou," Mr. Littledean said, standing straighter.

"He says he wants to show you around," Henry said as he opened the door.

"'O!" Mr. Littledean said, slapping a desktop firmly with the flat of his good hand.

"Yes, sir, I'm going!" Henry hurriedly closed the door behind him.

"Mer Wal-us, cle-n!"

Mr. Wallace looked helplessly at Adam. "What does he want?"

"I believe he wants you to clean up this mess."

"Wayesh," Mr. Littledean said.

He shuffled toward the door to the factory courtyard as Mr. Wallace piled ledgers into Walton Smythe's arms to return to the account's cupboard.

Mr. Littledean opened the door with his good hand. Looked back at Mr. Wallace and Mr. Smythe, nodded firmly, and escorted Adam into the factory courtyard.

"Very good, sir. Like I said for myself this morning. Go as you mean to carry on."

"Wayesh. Na, her ii pay-ing," he said.

"Painting department," Adam guessed, seeing the stacks of unadorned pottery and pots of paints.

Adam followed Mr. Littledean into the painting room. Fragile, unfired clay vessels, plates and statues stood in stacks on tables, and on shelves, with a few larger pieces on the floor. Adam worried he'd brush against a piece and send it crashing. He eased through the narrow aisles, following Mr. Littledean. Even with his awkward gait, Mr. Littledean moved easily through the maze.

Different painters raised their paint brushes in salute, but quickly returned to the tasks at hand. Adam watched one man spin a vase on a turntable and deftly lay down an even, thin stripe of color. He made it look easy. Adam shook his head and followed Mr. Littledean to a small alcove in a back corner.

Over Mr. Littledean's shoulder, Adam could see that there was a man sitting in the corner, fast asleep.

Mr. Littledean touched his arm. The man squirmed and resettled into position without opening his eyes. "I told you not to bother me!"

Adam watched Mr. Littledean's face twist into a lopsided frown. "Mer Hum-fe." He touched the man's arm.

"Dammit, Marie, I told you not to bother me," exploded the man seated in the chair. He jerked upright, swinging his arms as his eyes opened.

One swinging arm caught Mr. Littledean in the chest. Mr. Littledean stumbled backward against a table loaded with painted ware, sending pieces crashing to the floor. Adam rushed forward to catch Mr. Littledean before he crashed to the floor as well.

"Oh! Mr. Leetledean," a woman said, rushing forward to help.

"Mr. Littledean, sir!" exclaimed the man who'd been asleep. "So sorry sir, I didn't think to see you, I was just resting after lunch--"

"Just resting?" the woman who stooped to pick up broken pottery pieces said. "You sleep so deep you not hear us cheer Mr. Leetledean when he comes. Bah!"

"Shut up Frenchie and clean up that mess," the man said viciously, "Less I kick you out of here on that skinny backside." He looked up at Mr. Littledean. "Them Frenchies is talented but almost not worth putting up with their troublemaking mouths," he said.

Adam raised an eyebrow at the man's manner as he helped Mr. Littledean regain his balance.

"Ou—d!" Mr. Littledean shouted.

"What?" the man said.

"Ou—d!" Mr. Littledean roared louder. He pointed to the door.

"He said, *Out*," Adam told him. "Which means, *get out*. He is far nicer than me, I would say *Get the bloody hell out and don't let me see your beady-eyed face again!*"

"Wayesh," Mr. Littledean said, nodding. "Tan-u, Mer Wa-bur."

"You can't talk to me like that!" the man yelled at Adam. "I've been with Littledean's for nigh on twenty years."

"Probably five years too long," Adam returned.

"Make that fifteen years," Helena said caustically from the doorway. "What's happened?" she asked.

"S--eep," her father said.

"Ah, yes, he does that," Helena said.

"Your father tried to wake him. The man assumed he was someone named Maria and pushed him away." Adam gestured to the table. "Thus, the catastrophe with the wares. This woman came to pick up the pieces, and he yelled at her to clean up the mess lest he kick her out of the factory. Your father told him to get out."

Helena looked at her father. "You did? Good for you!" she enthused, crossing to give her father a hug. She stepped back. "So why is he still here?"

"I do not know," Adam said.

Helena glared at the man. "My father has told you to get out."

The man snarled at her. "Plenty of other potteries in town that will take a man with my experience." He trudged back to his desk.

"Where do you think you are going? That is not the direction to the door," Helena said.

"To get my things, girlee."

"The formulas!" said the woman from the floor. She stood up suddenly, her apron full of broken shards. "He breaks into Mr. Bickley's safe for the formulas."

"I did not, you lying Frenchie slut," Mr. Humphries said, raising his hand to backhand her.

Adam caught his arm, twisting it behind his back. He stiff-armed marched Humphries out the door and through the courtyard to the street.

"Damn you," Mr. Humphries struggled, "You can't steal my things!"

"They will be sent to you with your last wages. I assume Mr. Wallace has your correct direction?"

"Who are you?" Humphries ground out.

"Miss Littledean's fiancé." Adam let go of him, pushing him forward as he did so. He stood there a moment to ensure the man would walk away.

He decided he liked the sound of "Miss Littledean's fiancé." He knew Helena thought of it as a fake betrothal. Adam did not. But how to convince her he really wished to marry her? He thought of her often on the trip to Staffordshire. He knew for sure when she walked him to her room last night. Actually, he couldn't imagine any other woman as his wife, and he did not know how that had occurred. But it had, the certainty growing with each hour. He grinned to himself, then returned to the interior of the factory.

~

"Has he left?" Helena asked Adam when he came back to the painting department.

"Yes, but I don't trust him not to do some mischief," Adam said.

Helena's shoulders slumped a bit. "I don't either. It is sad, really. In his time, he was an excellent painter."

"His eyes, Miss Littledean," Miss Velois said. "The

eyes get bad, too bad for the fine line. His hands, they shake. He get mad. At everything, everyone. All he do is eat, sleep, and yell."

"Hou lon—?" Helena's father asked.

"How long has he been like this?" Helena translated.

Miss Velois shrugged apologetically. "Since before Mr. Leetledean gets sick."

"Be-fa?" Mr. Littledean said. "Wha?"

Helena turned back to Miss Velois. "He wants to know why this was never brought to his attention?"

She shrugged again. "Because we take care of our-selves?" she offered as an excuse, twisting her apron in her hands.

"You mean you took care of everyone," Helena said.

She looked down, not answering.

"That be true, miss, Mr. Littledean," said one painter working on an intricate statue. He pushed his flat gray cap back on his head. "Miss Velois watches out for us, makes sure we got paints and right colors. Gets the stencils, makes sure we got good brushes."

Helena grabbed one of Miss Velois' hands between her gloved ones. "You are a treasure. We—well, *I* at least—will see you rewarded."

Walton Smythe ran into the painting room. "Mr. Littledean, Mr. Franklin's returned with the banker, Mr. Shiskind," he gasped out, panting.

Mr. Littledean nodded. "Gou—"

He waved to Adam and Helena to follow him as he walked quickly through the painting room to the courtyard and back to the office.

A deep foreboding gripped Helena. She knew, more than anyone else, how important Mr. Shiskind's approval of them and their plans were. He could decide her father to be incompetent to manage the business, and with Mr. Bickley gone, could determine the Littledean Fine Porcelain factory was bound to implode with debts.

An engagement to the Earl of Norwalk was a lovely fantasy. It was something she would remember for the rest of her life, and the hours of bliss it engendered. Now reality was coming to overwhelm her. So much for dreams and aspirations. She inhaled deeply and drew up her reserves. She could get through this.

They found Mr. Shiskind sitting at the desk in Mr. Bickley's former office. He was a slender man of indeterminate years. An unremarkable man save for his beaked nose which dominated his appearance. He wore black with a dark burgundy and black jacquard waistcoat. His coat collar came up high alongside his head.

"Mer Shi—s--nd," Mr. Littledean said as he walked into the office. He sat down at the desk across from him. It amazed Helena at how confident and self-assured her father appeared, despite his mangled speech.

The banker raised an eyebrow. "I beg your pardon?"

"He said your name," Mrs. Littledean said austerely.

Helena privately cringed. Her mother was once again in her daughter of a duke mode.

"The apoplexy affected his speech and his right arm," her mother continued. "Not his mind. I, my daughter, or Mr. Franklin will translate anything you do not understand."

He frowned. "I'm not accustomed to discussing business with women."

"That is an attitude you will need to change, for the world is changing," said Adam.

"Who are you?" demanded Mr. Shiskind.

"Adam Waterbury. I handle the business affairs of the Earl of Norwalk estate in Devon."

Mr. Shiskind's eyes narrowed. "Aren't you far from the Norwalk properties?"

"I'm here to conduct business with Mr. Littledean."

"Hmph. We'll see." He turned to Mr. Littledean. "We've done business together for over twenty years."

"Wayesh," Mr. Littledean said, leaning back confidently in his chair. "So, wa ar- ewe wi—ho-ld f-un-s fum mer Wal-us?" he demanded."

Mrs. Littledean came to her husband's side. "He said, *So, why are you withholding funds from Mr. Wallace?*"

Mr. Littledean looked up at his wife and nodded. He turned again to Mr. Shiskind.

Mr. Shiskind looked at Mrs. Littledean. "This is dashed awkward."

"Don't tell me. It is him you need to talk to. After all, you don't talk business with women."

Helena saw a slight blush stain his neck and cheeks above the high coat collar.

"Don't be an impertinent woman," the banker snapped.

Mr. Littledean's chair scraped the floor as he pushed it back to get up. Mrs. Littledean forestalled him by laying her hand lightly on his arm.

"You haven't answered Mr. Littledean's question," Adam reminded the banker.

"I have a duty to protect the bank's investors. I must be certain that we are doing business with solid businessmen."

"Has Mr. Littledean ever given you reason to believe he is not solid in the year since his health issue?" Adam asked.

"No, but neither did I have any idea as to the severity of his incapacitation until someone told me."

"What besides his right arm and his speech is incapacitated?"

"I don't know, and that has me concerned. His mind could be addled. Some peoples' become so."

Mr. Littledean scowled. Helena was about to protest; however, Adam forestalled her by touching her arm. She looked at him.

He nodded at Mr. Shiskind. "I will grant you that; however, he has been running Littledeans ever since his health incident. It is my understanding Miss Littledean acted as his emissary, discussing decisions with Mr. Bickley and with her father."

"But Mr. Bickley is dead and there is no one else here."

"My husband is here, Mr. Shiskind. And he will continue to be here. Mr. Franklin will act as his secretary and translator for those who cannot listen closely enough to understand what he is saying."

Helena looked down so her face wouldn't betray a reaction to her mother's sniping words. She'd never seen her mother so forthright.

But before Mr. Shiskind could answer, the door to the front office opened. Helena recognized Mr. Lympne and Mr. Cheadley, two of the coal merchants that supplied coal for the bottle ovens.

Mr. Littledean rose from his chair to come out into the main room to greet them.

"Mer Lym-ne, Mer Shed-le, wel-kon."

"Josiah!" Mr. Lympne exclaimed. "Don't stand on formality with me. It's good to see you sir!"

"The same," said Mr. Cheadley.

"Heard you were back from Devon. We thought you might come here, what with Mr. Bickley gone."

"Wayesh," Mr. Littledean said.

Mr. Lympne shook his head. "Nasty business, very nasty business. Can't believe someone would murder Mr. Bickley. Well liked gentleman. You were lucky to have him."

"Wayesh."

"Came to talk about payment for coal. Mr. Shiskind has not been accepting Mr. Wallace's authorization of payment."

"Wha?" Mr. Littledean said. He swung around to look at Mr. Shiskind. "Nau Pay? Why?" he asked.

Mr. Shiskind looked from Henry to Mrs. Littledean.

"Yes," Mr. Cheadley chimed in. "Why haven't you authorized payment?" he asked. He frowned. "Is Littledean's having money issues?"

"No, no," Mr. Shiskind assured him. "However, that was because of Mr. Bickley. With Mr. Bickley's demise, as one of the bank's investors pointed out to me, Mr. Wallace is not authorized to make withdrawals. I need to be assured funds are seriously spent and my investors need confidence that Littledean's is properly run and managed."

Adam crossed his arms over his chest. "Would the investor who raised questions about Mr. Littledean's capabilities and Mr. Wallace's authority, be Mr. Firkins?"

"Why yes, it was. He is a large investor in the bank, so of course he has an interest in our solvency."

"And his company is also a competitor of Littledean's Fine Porcelain."

Mr. Lympne and Mr. Cheadley cried foul while the Littledeans looked at Mr. Shiskind in surprise.

"And did he also tell you, or infer, there would be new management, like perhaps his son, here at Littledean's?"

The banker nodded, his brow furrowing. "He mentioned his son had aspirations for Miss Littledean's hand in marriage and observed that would solve many problems."

"I would not marry Tibault Firkins if he were the last man on earth!" Helena cried out, her whole body shaking with anger.

"Ma dau-r wil na ma-r-e Fir-ns," Mr. Littledean declared. "I wo-od se-l bef-o hat!"

"How underhanded and deceitful!" Mrs. Littledean said. She put her arm around her daughter's shoulder. "It's a good thing you are already betrothed."

Mr. Shiskind looked at them. "What did he say?"

"He said, *My daughter will not marry Firkins. I would sell before that*," Henry helpfully provided.

"Good man!" cheered Mr. Cheadley.

"You are betrothed, Miss Littledean? Congratulations," Mr. Lympne said. "And who is the lucky man to be," he said gallantly.

"I am," Adam told the coal merchants. He turned back to Mr. Shiskind. "Now. Do you wish it known that you are working with someone to undermine the Littledean Fine Porcelain Company? What would that knowledge do to your pool of depositors?"

"Well, I can tell you right now, I'd move my money to Chubb's Bank," Mr. Lympne said. "If he would do this to Littledean, he could do that to any of us."

"Agreed," Mr. Cheadley said.

"No! No!" Mr. Shiskind protested. "I just needed to see for myself that Littledean's was being managed. It is obvious Mr. Firkins is misguided." He ran a finger along the rim of his collar, pulling at it.

"Misguided?" Helena exclaimed. "He's greedy, is what he is. He's jealous. Littledean's received a patten from the Queen for a tea service. He wants it and to have that he'd have to get Littledean's, but he is not willing to offer my father what the company is worth. He hopes to get it cheaply."

Mr. Shiskind frowned deeply. "I see," he said slowly. "Well," he said, pulling on his jacket to straighten it, "shall we add Mr. Wallace to the authorized for withdrawals list, Mr. Littledean?"

"Wayesh, an ma sec-re, Mer Fan-kin."

"He said, *Yes, and my secretary, Mr. Franklin.* That would be me," Henry told him helpfully.

Helena clapped her hands. "Excellent!"

"Now, we mus- see- hese genl-me pai —d so we ca —n ge— da bo— le ov —ns go— in," directed Mr. Littledean.

"*Now we must see these gentlemen paid so we can get the bottle ovens going,*" parroted Henry.

Mr. Littledean led Mr. Shiskind back to his office.

Helena nodded and smiled at him. Maybe there would be a chance for her to get back to her sculpting.

Adam turned to Mr. Lympne and Mr. Cheadley. "I never met Mr. Bickley. While we wait for Mr. Littledean and Mr. Shiskind to complete their business so you can get paid, can you tell me what was this gentleman like? The Littledeans thought highly of him."

Mr. Cheadley nodded. "And so they should. Fine young man. Well liked, I'd say. But very cautious."

"How do you mean cautious?" Adam asked.

"Well now, that be hard to say exactly. I just don't think he trusted anyone."

"If you want my opinion, something happened to him in the past that made him a watcher," Mr. Lympne said.

Mr. Cheadley nodded. "Had lots of friends, but no good friends. And he was slow to make decisions."

"That's true," Helena said. "We should have done something about Mr. Humphries long ago, but he didn't want to think about replacing him. And after Mr. Richmond died, he didn't want to replace him either right away, thought we should wait a bit, and I'll own he convinced me that was the right course of action, much to the consternation of Mr. Stringer who hoped to be promoted. I think it was the thought of replacing Mr. Stringer if we promoted him to Factory Manager, or Mr. Humphries as head of the painting department that made him bilious. Too much change, he would moan in a comical way."

Mr. Lympne laughed. "I'd not thought about how he could say no and make it into a joke for everyone to laugh about."

"Yes, he had the facility," Helena agreed. "I hadn't considered he had something bad happening in his past that caused him to be so careful, but you are correct, Mr. Cheadley."

"Interesting," Adam said. "May I ask you gentlemen, when was the last time you saw or spoke to Mr. Bickley?"

"Day 'afore he died," said Mr. Lympne, "we discussed coal deliveries and schedules."

"I saw him the day he died, at the Clay Pigeon where he meets with that group of earnest young men to discuss management."

"That was likely just a few hours, at most, before he died. Did he seem at all unhappy, or angry or anything like that?" Adam asked.

Mr. Cheadley shook his head. When the group was breaking up he was asked if he would join a few of them at the Hunting Dog for a last pint. I heard him tell them no, said he wanted to walk a bit to clear his head. Said he thought he'd imbibe a mite too much. As far as I could tell, alcohol did not bother him. Didn't drink much. Seldom did. But he was a bit pensive."

"That's right," Mr. Cheadley said.

"Is The Clay Pigeon far from where he was found?"

Mr. Cheadley shook his head. "Not far, but a mite twisty to get there from the pub. That's a working path for the horses and men pulling the barges up and down the river. Not a place for a pleasant stroll, if you catch my meaning."

"Yes, I think I do," Adam said.

Helena nodded as well.

They all heard the scraping of chairs against the rough wood floor of the office. Mr. Littledean and Mr. Shiskind were undoubtedly done with their meeting.

Mr. Shiskind handed notes to the coal merchants. "Bring these letters to the bank tomorrow and you will get your funds."

Both gentlemen voiced thanks and appreciation. Mr. Shiskind waved them aside. He turned back to Mr. Littledean. "I shall see you again tomorrow," Mr. Shiskind said, setting his hat on his head.

"Gentlemen, Madame, Miss, pleasure," he said, bowing stiffly.

Helena raised her hand to hide a smile at that last statement, which she knew to be anything but a pleasure. Ever the correct banker.

They watched the man leave.

CHAPTER 14
SCENE OF THE CRIME

"Is it true? Is it true?" George Stringer's strident voice cracked as he thrust the door between the factory courtyard and the office open. It banged against the shelving along the wall, rattling displayed porcelain and ceramic pieces.

"Mr. Stringer!" Mrs. Littledean admonished. "Careful."

"Pardon, ma'am," the man said in a rush. "Is it true? They're sayin' in the factory as how Mr. Humphries's been given the go!"

"Wayesh," Mr. Littledean said, rising from his chair again.

"Mr. Littledean, sar!" Mr. Stringer exclaimed. He rushed across the room to grasp his curled, paralyzed hand to pump it up and down.

Henry reached over and gently disengaged Mr. Stringer's hand from Mr. Littledean's.

"So glad to see you, sar!"

"Wayesh," Mr. Littledean said, stepping back, though he smiled lopsidedly at the man's enthusiasm.

"Mer Sin—er, fak-ery man—jer."

"Congratulations," Henry said.

"What?" Mr. Stringer said, looking between Henry and Mr. Littledean.

"Yes, congratulations," Helena enthused.

"If I'm not mistaken," Adam said, "I think you've just been promoted."

"What? No!"

"Wayesh," repeated Mr. Littledean, nodding and smiling.

"Well deserved, too," offered Mrs. Littledean.

"Oh, my—oh, my!" Mr. Stringer repeated. His gray eyes teared up as he clasped his palms against his cheeks. He collapsed down on a clerk stool in front of one of the high desks, then he jerked upright again.

"I'll do a good job, for you, sar. You won't regret this!" he told Mr. Littledean.

He looked like he was going to rush up to grasp Mr. Littledean's hand again until Mrs. Littledean stepped slightly between them.

Mr. Littledean nodded. "I kno—. Gou—j-ob."

"He said, *I know. Good job*," Henry said.

Mr. Stringer nodded, still dazed. "Well, well!" he said, "I'd best get out to the floor then!" he said, walking slowly to the door. With his hand on the door latch, he turned back.

"Thank you, sar! Lots to do!" He flung open the door, sending it banging against the shelves again. "Sorry!" he said, his face cringing and his shoulders hunching up to his ears. He went out the door and softly closed it behind him.

Helena laughed. "He is as giddy as a child with a new toy. He has long wanted that job."

"Why hasn't he been promoted before this?" Adam asked, looking at Mr. Littledean.

Mr. Littledean shook his head and looked back at his daughter.

Helena sighed. "After Mr. Richmond died, Mr. Bickley didn't want to fill the factory manager position right away. He wanted to learn it first. I agreed with his idea that learning the jobs of the managers was important for him as general manager. He thought he'd have the best opportunity to learn by taking on the factory manager tasks as well."

Mrs. Littledean frowned. "Taking on both General Manager and Factory Manager? That is too much for one person in a factory our size."

Helena shrugged a little, her lips pulling up on the right side. "I helped," she confessed.

Her mother laughed. "Of course, you would have! But did you help, or did you take on one of the jobs."

"Oh, no!" Helena protested.

"Near enough!" said Mr. Wallace from his stool on the other side of the high desks. "I don't know how much he learned of the factory as you ran most of that, for all you say he wanted to learn."

Her father and mother laughed, and even Adam joined in.

"Why am I not surprised?" Adam said, shaking his head and looking up at the ceiling.

"Mer Wal— sh, co—m to the of—ish. Pl—s," said Mr. Littledean.

"Mr. Wallace," Henry said, "Mr. Littledean would like you to come to the office."

"Wayesh," said Mr. Littledean.

"Oh! Yes, of course." Mr. Wallace got off the high stool and put on a brown jacket hanging on a hook behind him.

Helena turned to Adam. "I was going to take you around for a tour of the factory since our previous attempt went only so far as the painting department, but I don't think now is the time to continue that. We need

to let Mr. Stringer have his time with his new employees."

"Wayesh," said her father nodding.

"That place where Mr. Bickley was killed, is it far
from here?" Adam asked.

"No," chimed in Walton from his high stool. "Just
twisty to get there. I could lead you there, now if you'd
like."

Mr. Wallace stopped at the office door. "No, you
can't," he said. "We've bills to pay and invoices to write
now that Mr. Littledean has set up things with the
banker. You can get started with those while I meet
with Mr. Littledean. When you are done with those,
you may leave for the day."

Walton pouted and seemed to shrink in on
himself.

"How is it you know the location?" Helena asked
when her parents, Henry, and Mr. Wallace had closed
the office door behind them.

"From my middle brother, Marcus. It were his best
mate, Eddie, as found Mr. Bickley."

"The magistrate said he was found by the canal."

"Yes. You know the stone bridge that has the canal
path running under it then climbs the bank to run
along the top of the bank again? The one Mr. Grundy
hides under from Mrs. Grundy when he's had too
much to drink?"

Helena laughed. "Yes."

"Eddie told Toby that right where the path gets
back to the top of the bank, all the tall grasses were
bent. He thought maybe Mr. Grundy didn't make it to
his sobering place and rolled down the hill toward the
canal. He looked down to see if Mr. Grundy needed
some help."

Walton hunched forward, getting into his tale.

"He saw Mr. Bickley. He said he slid down the hill to come beside him," he mimed sliding off the stool, "and found him stone cold *dead*!" he said with emphasis. "He had blood all over his neckcloth, flies and crawly bugs in the blood and all over him," he enthused, making crawling motions with his fingers on his own neck and over his face. "And them big buzzard birds were circling up above," he finished, waving a hand up above his head in a circle.

Helena shivered. "Gracious, Mr. Smythe, you could be a writer like my cousin!" she suggested, thinking of the dark, gothic mysteries her cousin Lancelot wrote as *Anonymous*.

"Well," Walton said, pushing lanky dark blond hair out of his eyes, "Eddie said it was gruesome. I went there myself and saw the bent grass and blood there, but the magistrate's men had come and collected the body, so I missed that. Course rains washed all the blood away since then," he said complacently.

"Of course," Adam agreed. "Still, I should like to see the area for myself."

"To what purpose?" Mrs. Littledean asked.

"I don't know," he confessed.

"A boy's morbid curiosity?" she teased.

He laughed. "I don't know. Maybe that is all it is." He turned toward Helena. "Think you could show me where it is?"

She shrugged. "Yes."

"And could we go by the Clay Pigeon?"

"Where he had dinner with his friends?" she asked.

"Yes," he said.

She nodded. "It would be on our route to the stone bridge."

"It is unfortunate you didn't bring Dessie with you today."

"Why?"

"What is more above reproach than a gentleman escorting a lady while she walks her dog?"

Helena laughed. "Don't concern yourself with my reputation. I am neither peerage nor gentry." She cocked her head back. "Besides, aren't we supposed to be betrothed?"

"Yes," he said, "And, there is nothing supposed about it."

IT SURPRISED Adam how close to the Littledean Fine Porcelain factory the Clay Pigeon Pub stood. At the south edge of the factory property across a road that led into the town in one direction into the countryside in the other, stood a hand-hewn stone block building with mullioned windows. Some on the ground floor appeared quite ornate, like one might see in a church. Iron tracery edged the window peaks jutting from a roof graced with a dark gray slate.

It was the kind of pub that had stood at the cross-roads for centuries, welcoming weary travelers and local day labor.

They stopped in front of the pub.

Helena nodded her head toward the bow window before them. "On the other side of that window is a large round table. That is where Mr. Bickley and his peers would meet for dinner. They would watch the world go by and gossip as furiously as old women about the people who passed by," Helena told Adam as they stood in front of the pub, her arm tucked into the crook of his arm.

"How do you know this? Did you attend the dinners?" he asked, looking down at her, his glorious gold eyes shadowed by the brim of his beaver hat.

She laughed. "Gracious, no. Mr. Bickley told me. It was not a venue for a woman, or so he advised me."

"I can tell by your tone that you think little of that edict,"

"Hardly, but it is what it is. I believe these rules will evolve over the fullness of time," she said, smiling enigmatically.

"Women ruling the world?"

"Not so men would know," Helena responded.

Adam looked at her, puzzled, then he frowned and raised one eyebrow while his lips flattened into a tight line.

Helena laughed, and despite himself, Adam laughed back.

"I don't know why I looked askance at you. That is something my father would do. As much as I try to divest myself of his teachings, some still jerk out like a knee that is rapped might, despite the contrary teachings from my mother. You had little an opportunity to get to know my mother when you visited, as short as the visit was."

"No," she admitted.

He smiled. "My mother generated, and continues to generate, a fortune by investing in new technologies and scientific breakthroughs," he said proudly. "My father was disastrously jealous of her ability but refused to take her advice, as he thought a woman could never understand science and industry. To his mind, she'd been lucky and that luck, as he saw it, drove him mad. That is why my parents were estranged, my mother having her own household, carriage, and horses."

Helena suddenly realized they were being re-
garded by patrons inside the pub. "Let's continued
on," she said.

He agreeably led her further down the lane.

They walked along a rail fence for some thirty to
forty feet. A thick, dark green hedgerow soon replaced
the wood fence. An independent, stubborn vine with
small, colorful flowers grew through the hedgerow.
The smell was enticing, but Adam didn't know what it
was. Beyond the hedgerow were a few small brick and
stone homes of pottery workers. The hedgerow
thinned and disappeared the closer they came to the
canal.

The towpath that ran parallel to the canal was
hard packed and free of ruts and large stones. They
turned to the right to follow the towpath.

"The canals were built some forty to fifty years ago
to facilitate transporting pottery goods to city mar-
kets," she explained.

"How does a canal facilitate transportation?"

"There are no ruts as there are in a road, so it cuts
down on breakage."

"Interesting." he said.

"Not this first bridge, but bridge after is the one
Walton spoke of," Helena said as they followed the
path under the near bridge and alongside the canal.

"It doesn't appear that he had to walk far, looks ap-
plicable for an evening stroll after an enormous meal."

Helena thought about that. "Yes, save for the various nipping insects that come out near the water as
the sun sets."

The path continued along the water's edge. In the
sunlight, the bodies of the insects glinted as they
darted about. They soon came to the second bridge,
where they claimed Mr. Grundy hid from his wife. On

the other side, Helena pulled her arm free from his so she might gather her block printed cotton skirts, to make it easier to ascend the slight rise on the other side of the bridge.

Adam steadied her from behind as she climbed the rise.

Helen felt out of breath when they got to the top. And Helen knew it wasn't from the exertion. She yet felt the ghost of the palm of his hand resting against the small of her back. It sent delightful tremors through her, tremors she dared not succumb to. She was attracted to Adam far more than she cared to admit, and not because he resembled the painting in her studio. That was a boy. The body standing next to her was that of a man. Her breath came a little faster. She willed it to slow as she looked about the area, screened from the canal and the rest of the towpath both ahead and behind by the large trees that shaded the area, along with the shrubs, grasses and flowering vines that grew riotously at the edge of the path.

It was a delightful fantasy to think of marrying Adam Waterbury, Earl or not. She'd fallen quickly in love with the man.

Too quickly.

It had to be false. For what did she know of love? She'd seen the affection between her parents, but must one have love to have affections? Affection could come from friends as well. Couldn't it? These sensations that thrilled her when he stood near confused her. She'd never experienced their like before. It was worth being wary.

She couldn't trust her emotions. Too much had been happening too quickly. Her parents were counting on her to help with the factory. Her father could suffer another apoplexy at any time. Today, tomorrow, next month, never? Who could say? What would happen to her mother if he did?

She could not think of the lovely feelings that pulsed through her at Adam's touch. She smiled to herself when she realized she now thought of him as Adam, whereas she had told him just that morning that to think of Adam would only put her in mind of the painting. The name no longer did so. She only thought of the man. How had that come about?

She turned toward him, surprised to find how close he stood as he studied the landscape where Mr. Bickley was found. She noticed the warmth emanating from his body and his unique scent that she wanted to bathe in.

"If this is where Mr. Bickley was killed, I doubt anyone would have seen anything save the murderer himself," she said. She would have taken a step back; however, he put his arm around her and drew her closer.

"Yes," he murmured. "It is hidden." He lowered his head slowly, then touched her lips with his.

A sharp intake of breath was her only reaction before his lips pressed firmly against hers. Helena found her arms floating upward, seemingly of their own volition, to wrap about his neck. She rose on her toes as she returned his kiss.

He drew her closer to him, her feet leaving the ground as he clasped her body against his. She felt his manhood strain against his falls.

Shivers shook her body, and a warm dampness claimed her nether region.

Shocked, she pushed against him.

He let her go.

"No," she said with a strangled cry. "Please, no."

"No? But why, my sweet. I can tell you want me as much as I want you."

"No, it can't be," she said, tears silently falling.

"What is it?" His eyes searched her face. He brought his hands up to gently cup her face, his thumbs wiping at the tears under her eyes.

"It has been a lovely fantasy to dream of being with you," she said. "But I can't."

"Why?"

"We come from such different worlds. I don't fit in to yours."

"Neither did your parents, and they have made it work."

She laughed a little. "I don't have the social assurance my mother possesses. And even with the assurance, she is not comfortable with what she sees as the artifice of society. She says it is too much, and so I think it is for me as well. The Malmsby relations are a boisterous lot, teasing, pulling pranks. I always feel like an outsider." She turned around and leaned back against him. "My grandmother is the worst. I love her dearly; however, if she knew I had your picture, I should get unmercifully teased."

"All the more reason to give the picture to me so I can get rid of it and she need never know."

"I can't do that," she whispered. "I can't explain it precisely; however, I feel that painting has given me strength over the years to do what I have had to do. I have no desire to be a businesswoman like your mother. I would rather be a sculptress."

"And perhaps a wife and mother?" he said into her ear.

She smiled. "Yes, and those, too, but those are dreams as well."

She turned back around and placed her hands flat

on his chest. "You know, my father could suffer another apoplexy, and the next might be fatal. I can't leave my mother to deal with that and the factory as well. Though she and your mother maybe great friends, they are very different."

He tucked one of the flyaway strands of hair back under her bonnet. "My mother is even now working on a long-term solution to protect against that event, for you must know, it is not a matter of if, but more of when."

She looked down, and tears flowed again. "I know, though I try to keep that locked away in the deepest, darkest regions of my mind, not to see the light of day."

He pulled her toward him again, his touch different now, gentle and sympathetic, the sensual caresses tucked away.

"I am a beast for stating it."

"No, for it is the truth and why I cannot allow myself to respond to you, no matter how strong the urge to melt into you is. I have never felt feelings like this before."

"And that is another reason I am a beast, for I know that, and I am taking advantage of you." He pulled his handkerchief from his pocket and blotted her tears away. "That is not how I wish to be," he said. "That is not the man I wish to be. You know, when I first met you, I thought you were like a fae creature, a fae princess. I was ensorcelled by you at that first meeting. You, together with Dessie, wove magic around me. And I swear around Foster as well!"

She laughed at that, a watery little chuckle.

"We will see this through. We will sort out Mr. Bickley's death, and we will get your father a new partner, or help him sell the business, whichever he chooses. You should have your own life. You know that is what they want for you, don't you? They do not want you to live just for them and the factory. If they did, they would have encouraged a match with that Mr. Thirkens, of Firkins, or whatever his name is."

Helena inhaled deeply. "There is truth in your words."

"Yes," he said lightly, "I'm more than just a nude man in a painting."

She looked up at him for a moment as what he said registered in her mind. A spurt of laughter came from her.

Then another.

Then another.

Soon she was giggling uncontrollably.

She hugged him fiercely, then stepped back. "Thank you for that. I needed a good laugh," she said as tears of laughter replaced the tears of sadness.

CHAPTER 15
WHAT WALTON KNOWS

"Did you have a pleasant walk with the Earl?" Mrs. Littledean asked her daughter as they rode in the carriage back to Tyche Manor, leaving Mr. Littledean at the factory to return with Henry Franklin and the earl later.

Helena smiled sadly. "Yes," she said softly.

"Why the sad expression?"

"I am strangely enamored of him and it's a fantasy!"

"What is?"

"What do you mean, what is? The Earl and I as a couple, of course."

"Why is it a fantasy? If it wasn't a fantasy for me to love your father, then it shouldn't be a fantasy for you to love the Earl of Norwalk."

"Our situations are different."

"How so?"

Helena shifted uncomfortably in her seat. "They are. Our lives are different. I know nothing about estates and estate management."

"Which you don't need to know."

"But that is the thing. I would wish to be a part of

the world I am in, not an—an appendage."

"Is that how you think of me? As an appendage in your father's world?"

"No!"

"Helena, you refine too much on the differences in your birth circumstances. What are you really afraid of?"

"I don't know what you mean."

Her mother looked at her severely. "I hope the only person you are lying to is me and not to yourself as well."

"Mother! I could never!"

"Do not throw up barriers where there are none."

"I have witnessed you draw a mantle about yourself of hauteur. You can project a snubbing, belittling arrogance that lets a person know they are less than the dirt beneath your feet. I'll admit, it is amusing to see you turn that air on others; however, I remember all too well at Mrs. Napleton's academy when that was how I was daily treated, with dismissive arrogance by the other girls and Mrs. Napleton. I was miserable there. I can't imagine willingly allowing myself to be set amongst people with that attitude once again. If I were to marry the earl, it would thrust me back into that reproving world. I have felt fortunate that I have been spared a London season. My lack of a season has made you and grandmother sad. I assure you; I am not! I shudder to think about how I might have been treated. I lack your confidence. The snickering comments I received from the girls at the school were too much."

"Helena! I did not know."

Her mother slid across the seat to envelop Helena in a hug.

"When I think of my actions from your position, I

am mortified! How cruel we are, how unthinkingly cruel!"

Tears welled in Mrs. Littledean's eyes. She pulled a handkerchief out of her reticule.

"Honestly, that arrogance I sometimes wrap around myself like a cloak when talking to people like Mr. Firkins, or Mr. Shiskind, is my way of hiding. As a woman, it is the one weapon I have readily at my disposal."

"I knew it was artifice; and I knew it was a weapon. I just assumed it was a weapon of strength. How fascinating that we should come at this from different angles."

Her mother reached over to squeeze Helena's hands where they lay in her lap.

"I can see how his world could be frightening. However, if you love each other, then it will all work out."

"How does one know when one is in love? What is the difference between love and fascination? How can I have known him long enough to be in love? Three days! And not even full days, with many days in between."

Her mother shrugged. "The heart knows. Most people don't have the opportunity to indulge the heart. That is not the way marriages are made. But for now, just enjoy the experience. Banns have not been read, and even if they were, vows have not been spoken. The only fact you need to understand is neither your father nor I will push you to a marriage you don't want."

The carriage drew up before their home. To their surprise, Mr. Drummond stood outside waiting for them. Beside him stood young Walton Smythe, his lank blond hair flopped over one eye, his cravat a tangled, wrinkled mess. Under his left arm, he carried a dark gray account book.

Mr. Drummond came forward as Mrs. Littledean descended from the carriage.

"Mrs. Littledean, Miss Littledean, please excuse this intrusion," he said, grasping Mrs. Littledean's hand between his two hands.

"You are never an intrusion, Mr. Drummond," Mrs. Littledean said, looking curiously between Mr. Drummond and Walton Smythe.

"Is Mr. Littledean due to return soon as well?" he asked when the carriage drove off for the stables without discharging any other passengers.

"Soon, yes. He wanted to do a factory walk-through before he returned home."

"Yes, yes, of course," Mr. Drummond said. He drew a large handkerchief from his coat pocket and mopped his brow. It was unusual to see the vicar in a state of distress.

"Please come into the house with us. I'll order tea," Mrs. Littledean said. "They should be back here soon."

"Thank you," the vicar said, stuffing his kerchief back in his voluminous coat pocket.

Helena walked into the house.

"Sutton, please arrange for tea and refreshments in the parlor," Mrs. Littledean said as she led the much-agitated vicar inside.

"Very good ma'am."

"And brandy as well," Helena added, looking over the vicar's appearance. "And some lemonade for Mr. Smythe," she added.

The vicar smiled wanly at the mention of brandy. "That would be appreciated. The world is flipped over. If this young man is to be believed, everything I thought I knew has been torn asunder. How does one go as a man of God?"

Mrs. Littledean laughed. "Since that is something I am not, nor ever will be, I can't answer that question for you, Mr. Drummond. But perhaps if you tell us, we might provide some help."

"Walton has brought to my attention some disturbing information about Mr. Bickley and his dealings with Mr. Stringer, Mr. Wallace, and others. Very disturbing. My mind is quite taken up with the facts as Mr. Smythe has presented them to me. I had to come to you immediately and relate these tidings."

"If it affects Littledean Fine Porcelain in a larger context, perhaps it would behoove us to wait for Mr. Littledean and the others.

Sutton entered with the brandy tray. Helena motioned him over to Mr. Drummond.

"Please, Mr. Drummond," Helena said, taking the poured brandy from Sutton and passing to the vicar, "Sip some brandy and try to relax."

"Yes, sound words, Miss Littledean. Sound words." His hand shook as he lifted a glass off the brandy tray. Helena and her mother exchanged glances.

The maid carried in the tea service with lemonade for Mr. Smythe.

"You are in luck, Mr. Smythe," Helena said conversationally. "We also have cinnamon cake today." She put a large piece on a plate and passed it to the boy, then poured him some lemonade.

He tossed his head to flip his hair back before he took the mug of lemonade. "Thank you, Miss!"

She paused in raising her teacup to her lips as she heard the wheels against the crushed rock drive before the house.

"Hopefully that will be the gentlemen returned

from the factory. Better for you to explain once than twice. Enjoy the cinnamon cake while you can, for once they see it, the slices will be gone," Helena advised.

Helena saw Walton look to Mr. Drummond for guidance; however, that gentleman was obviously fretting and not giving him his attention. She leaned over to the boy.

"Take two while you can. I'm serious. They will be devoured. Do not wait for permission."

Young Walton nodded eagerly and grabbed two of the largest pieces of the cake for his plate. Helena grinned approvingly.

"Whash go-in ahn," Mr. Littledean exclaimed demanded as he came through the parlor door.

Helena felt a thrill of excitement at her father's take charge manner, whether or not anyone understood him. It was a big change from the quiet man he'd become because of his infirmities. This, more than anything, proved he was recovering.

"What did he say?" asked Mr. Drummond.

"Oh, sorry, vicar. He asked what is going on."

"Young Mr. Smythe has some news to share with us about activities at the factory that Mr. Drummond feels is pertinent to learning more about Mr. Bickley's murder."

Mr. Littledean nodded as he took a seat next to his wife on the sofa. "Gou Laa." Mrs. Littledean handed him a plate with cinnamon bread.

"It's about Mr. Bickley, sir," the boy said. "I heard Mr. Wallace talk to you about what went on in the office while you were gone, and it weren't like Mr. Wallace said. Leastwise, not all ways. That bothered me so I told Mr. Drummond and he said as how I should explain to you."

"Gou, gou," Mr. Littledean said, leaning forward toward the boy.

"I hear you and others talk about how nice Mr. Bickley was and how everyone liked him. He scratched his head. I don't know how that could be, because that's not what I saw and heard."

He took a sip of his lemonade.

"With you gone, miss, he changed."

"What do you mean?"

"He wanted to argle-bargle with everyone. Even Miss Velois! All she wanted was one of those cards he had for a color, and he made her cry before he gave it to her."

"I thought he was sweet on her," Helena said.

"I think she did, too, but not after that day. He were nasty. And he and Mr. Wallace were always wrangling, especially about this book," he said, touching the gray ledger book beside him on the chair. Mr. Wallace was angry about something he found in the book. Mr. Bickley promised him half of whatever was recorded in the book.

"Blackmail?"

"I don't know, Miss, but Mr. Wallace were tight with the book, hardly letting it out of his sight. Then, when Mr. Bickley was killed, he relaxed. Even left it at the office. I don't know what was in the book that worried Mr. Wallace so, but I brung it," Walton said.

"Mr. Bickley also told Mr. Stringer there was no way he would get to be Factory Manager but would never tell Mr. Stringer why, though Mr. Stringer asked often enough."

"And what were odd," he said, his head canted to the side, "were that Mr. Firking came to the office to talk to Mr. Bickley and after he left, I heard Mr. Bickley clinking coins in his pocket over and over. He didn't do that afore the meeting. Mr. Wallace noted that, too, and said something. Mr. Bickley sniped it was none of his business. But not two hours later, they were out together and came back arm in arm. Best of mates, you know. I saw them out in the street before they entered the office. They were with the other Mr. Firkins. The younger one. Laughing and joking,"

"Did you hear anything they said?"

"No, but Mr. Firkins clapped them on the back and they shook hands. And when they came in, Mr. Wallace took this ledger," he picked up the gray ledger from where he'd tucked it behind him on the seat, "into Mr. Bickley's office and had Mr. Bickley make entries, not me."

"Mr. Drummond said as it how sounded not proper, that I should tell you."

"Oh, and another odd thing," the boy added. "Mr. Wallace was always friendly with Mr. Stringer until he went out with Mr. Bickley and Mr. Firkins, and after that, he started getting nasty with Mr. Stringer, too."

"What had Mr. Stringer done?"

He shook his head. "Can't say why exactly but I talked about it with Mr. Drummond. We think Mr. Stringer tries too hard to please everyone, and that's a bit tiresome habit."

Mr. Drummond nodded. "I've seen similar situations in my career with the church. Bullies like to discover a person's weak point, then magnify it all out of proportion with its actuality."

"Don't I know it!" Helena said spiritedly.

"How long has Mr. Bickley worked for Littledean Fine Porcelain?" Adam asked.

"Almost five years. He was recommended as an inventory clerk. We needed a better way to decide on what patterns we needed to replenish. He worked with our London agents and distributors in Bath and Edinburgh, and foreign exporters. In a brief time, he managed sales, and when Mr. Littledean had his apoplexy, he was made acting general manager."

"While he was a capable inventory manager and sales manager, he didn't shine as much as the general manager. He often spoke about how he felt uncertain if he was doing a good job. At first, he came to Tyche Manor to meeting with father a couple of times a week, then I started taking messages to him from father several times a week and in the last six months, I have been there every day. Mr. Bickley said he enjoyed having me there. It gave him confidence that he was doing as my father wished."

"Miss Littledean, did Mr. Bickley display any uncertainty to you?"

"Not if you recognized his accomplishments"

"Did you find you needed to give him recognition daily?"

"Give him recognition? No. Though he sometimes spoke of not being confident, he never displayed a lack of confidence. He always struck me as confident in what he did. Now, he was a bit shaky in his knowledge of the factory; however, we have a good staff. They are good at their trades. His strength lay with the sales and relationships built outside the company. And that was what we needed him to do. I never had the feeling he felt uncertain in that role. Why?"

"My mother has often lectured me on appreciation for our staff. She has long insisted that a nod, a smile, or some other small recognition can go a long way to improving worker productivity," Adam said.

"If he wasn't getting recognition, he may have turned to another sort of recognition, like from Mr. Firkins the elder and the younger."

"He was selling out Littledean for a few words of praise?" Helena asked incredulously.

"It is possible."

"That idea still doesn't bring us any closer to figuring out who killed him. Or why. All it proves is what I knew. I am not cut out to be a factory manager."

He smiled at her. "No, you are an artist. Managing the factory and Mr. Bickley is not playing to your strength. I believe you and Mr. Bickley complemented each other, but neither was satisfied with the situation."

"It's true I wasn't. I can't say for Mr. Bickley."

"I wish we had known that," her mother said. "I thought you enjoyed running the factory. You are certainly good at it."

"A small part of me did, and I felt proud of what I accomplished with Mr. Bickley, but it isn't my heart's desire. It isn't what gets me looking forward to the next day."

"What does that?" Adam asked.

"Thinking about my next sculpture. My next challenge."

Adam nodded. "For me, I enjoy making plans for the estate. To see it rise out of the ashes of my father's destruction."

"And I enjoy designing a new tea service," Mrs. Littledean admitted. "Something different that will capture the imagination of the ton and be a popular design. Isn't it interesting how we each have our driving forces? And that is how it should be. Mr. Smythe, what do you envision as your future driving force?"

"It won't be what Mr. Wallace does," Walton said earnestly. "Those columns of little numbers make my eyes go crossed. But Mr. Wallace, that is what he likes. He looks for patterns in numbers, he says. I don't see patterns in numbers. I don't mind the numbers, but not every day. That is not for me."

"Do you see patterns in something else?" Adam asked.

"Yes! How things can fit together."

"Mr. Smythe—Walton, might we see this ledger?" Mrs. Littledean asked.

"Yes, that is why I brought it. I don't understand what these notes are. They were entered at the back of the book. They are like entries I made at Mr. Wallace's direction. But entered here, they have different values. Or, some are different values."

"Dif—ent vol—u?" Mr. Littledean said.

Walton looked confused.

"Different values, Mr. Littledean is asking if he heard correctly," Mrs. Littledean said.

"Yes, sir. Different values. Like where Mr. Wallace had me enter 1.1 in the book's front as the price of a lot of stencils, In the back is recorded .95P."

"Skimming?" Helena asked.

"So it would appear; however, who would be foolish enough to record the skimming in the same book? Something doesn't add up. Mr. Smythe, where is this book typically kept?" Adam asked.

"If it is not in the locked ledger cupboard, Mr. Wallace keeps it to hand and often takes it home with him."

"How is it that it is not locked in the cupboard now?"

"He didn't lock it."

"Has he ever done that before? Forgotten to lock the cupboard?"

"No, sir. He's ever careful. Or leastwise always was until that day he came back with Mr. Bickley and Mr. Firkins. It was like he didn't care anymore."

"He probably didn't."

"This makes little sense.

"Tomorrow," Adam said, "I will study the books as part of my role as fiancé working on settlements."

Helena made a face. Adam laughed.

"You could help me," he suggested.

"Perhaps," she said.

"To-rd" Mr. Littledean said after Mr. Drummond and Mr. Smythe left.

"Yes, I imagine you are tired," Mrs. Littledean said. "This is the most active you have been in months. Why don't you lay down and rest before dinner."

"Wayesh," her husband said. There was a decidedly gray pallor to his face.

"I'll fetch Mr. Wolversham for you," Henry Franklin said, walking swiftly to the parlor door.

"Th-onk U."

The silence while they waited for Wolversham unnerved Helena. She needed to put some time and space between herself and the earl. Their feelings for each other had come too hard and too fast. She did not trust the feelings, though they felt heavenly. She needed to think. She needed to think about her family, her future, and the future of Littledean Fine Porcelain. For good or bad, they were inextricably bound. She had a duty to her family and her heritage that she could not simply walk away from and ignore. The newness of the feelings the Earl brought to her needed to be balanced. She was not a young and infatuated girl.

"This has been a day with much to think about. If you will excuse me, my lord," she said, addressing

Adam, "I would go to my studio," she said, suddenly needing to put distance between herself and the earl. "There is a lump of clay there I'm eager to work on," she said lightly. "That activity will calm my mind and hopefully put what I've heard today into clarity." *And help me see my way clearly.*

She curtsied and fled out of the room as the door opened to admit Mr. Wolversham. That worthy frowned at her running out the door. He shook his head dolefully and proceeded to Mr. Littledean's side. He and Henry Franklin helped Mr. Littledean from the parlor and upstairs to his room.

～

ADAM FINISHED his brandy and returned his glass to the tray.

"Why is it, Mrs. Littledean, that you have not appeared unduly perturbed by the revelations today?"

She sighed and shook her head. "It is not that I am unperturbed. I am perturbed. Deeply perturbed; however, your mother warned me of scenarios we might see occurring."

"Ah. She foretold the weakness in the hearts of men," Adam said dramatically, clapping a hand on his heart.

She chuckled. "Essentially, yes. It is difficult for a young man to make his way in industry unless he is born or married into it. And your mother has noted that it is galling to be the spare or somewhere in the spare chain. Not trained; however, if it comes their way, held to the same expectations we train the heir for in the role."

"I was originally the spare," he said drily. "I understand."

"Sorry, yes, I guess you do. When I wrote to her to inform her of Mr. Littledean's apoplexy, she asked what my plans were when —if—Mr. Littledean has another, worse attack."

"My mother can be blunt to a fault."

"Yes, but sometimes such candor is the best conversation to have."

He nodded, "True."

"Since that time, she has canvased her Gentlemen's Trade of younger sons club to discover if any would be interested in the ceramic and porcelain trade. She found a gentleman who was interested. He had an excellent education, paid for by his maternal grandmother, and he has an interest in chemistry. He did research on the industry, and reports he is impressed with the strides made in modernization over the last fifty years by potters such as Josiah Wedgwood — who was Mr. Littledean's godfather. Satisfied he might be a suitable candidate to succeed in our trade, she arranged for him to get a position at the Littledean Fine Porcelain showroom in London. He has been working there for the last five months, learning the customer side of the industry."

"That sounds like something my mother would do. Does Mr. Littledean know what my mother is doing?"

"Yes. He didn't like it at first. I believe he felt I was expecting him to die. But when he didn't make the recovery he wanted, he realized the difficulty from the creditability aspect. The banker's attitude today is something that did concern him as a possibility. Then, when clay was discovered on your property and we might have the first opportunity to buy it, he saw the overall benefits," she said with a laugh.

"But you haven't told your daughter," Adam said.

"No. I felt she might take that as a slight on her

abilities. Though she ostensibly helped Mr. Bickley, it has been her ideas that have driven the company forward over the last few months. My husband pulled back from giving advice. He has taken the position of asking what she thinks and then agreeing with her! We are proud of her."

Adam frowned and compressed his lips together as he thought of the few things Helena had said to him.

"Mrs. Littledean, I urge you tell her."

"Why?"

"Because I think she feels obligated to the factory through you."

"Nonsense."

"Is it?" he asked.

"Well, all will be clear soon enough. I am awaiting word from your mother now as to how soon her Gentlemen's Trade Club member might travel to Staffordshire to work with Mr. Littledean toward partnership.

He nodded. "She said she was looking into providing help. I didn't question her as to what form the help would take. I have had several of my university friends end up receiving the benefit of her business wisdom. Not all families have been appreciative of what she has done for their sons. But the sons are! My friend Hugh Talverton traveled to New Orleans to buy cotton for a new modern mill my mother was investing in. He ended up staying in the United States and marrying the daughter of a New Orleans cotton factor. He's done far better for himself than his own father would have. If you will excuse me, Mrs. Littledean, I need to write to my estate steward and some other correspondence."

"Of course, my lord. I look to see you at dinner."

CHAPTER 16

THE PAINTING

The shadows lengthened almost to darkness by the time Adam finished franking his last outgoing letter. He rang for the young man the Littledeans had assigned to his services during his visit and directed him to ensure his notes caught the next day's Express Mail. Even with Express Mail, the letters would take several days to reach their addressees.

He wandered downstairs again and asked the butler where he might find Miss Littledean.

"At this hour before dinner, Miss Littledean is often in her studio, my lord."

"Can you direct me to the studio?" he asked.

"Certainly. It is in the west wing. If you will follow me, my lord," Mr. Sutton said, leading him down a long hall that ran between the formal and informal parlors.

Adam found the hall they traversed strangely devoid of artwork. Its plain, light cream-colored walls were lined with red oak cabinets fitted with glass doors. As he passed the cabinets, he noted they were filled with porcelain statues of dogs, cats, and various forest animals created with a delicate attention to de-tail in their form, their surroundings, and in their color glaze.

"Were these prototypes of factory pieces?" he asked Mr. Sutton.

"Some. Most are learning pieces of the young miss."

"Learning pieces? Some of these are exquisite!"

"Yes, my lord," agreed Mr. Sutton as they continued down the hall.

"What is she doing working in a factory when she could make pieces like this?"

"I couldn't say, my lord," the butler returned flatly, though Adam had a feeling the man would say much more under other circumstances.

"I understand, Mr. Sutton."

The butler paused and turned to look at Adam.

"Thank you, my lord," he said. "That door on the right is the entrance to the young miss's studio."

"I appreciate you guiding me here. No need to announce me."

"Very good, my lord," Mr. Sutton said as he bowed. He turned on his heel and walked back to the main part of the house.

Adam stood outside the closed door. What should he say to her? What could he tell her? It wasn't his place to tell her what her mother said to him; however, he knew her lack of knowledge could lead her away from him. Did he hope that her newfound love for him could lead her to him despite what she thought she needed to do for her parents?

To do so would be to both their sorrows. Yet could he break a mother's confidence? Did her mother know her better? Were the thoughts she confessed to him real, or her trying them on as one would try on a jacket to see if it fit?

He raised his chin up and stared at the ceiling for a moment as he wrestled with himself.

He needed to trust that her mother knew her better than he did.

He rapped lightly on the door and heard a muffled "Come in," in return.

Helena stood with her back to him at a worn oak worktable with a large block of clay before her on a flat turning wheel. A collection of wire and steel tools, some mounted in wood handles, lay haphazardly about, some stood stacked neatly upright in a plain gray ceramic pot.

"Is it dinnertime, already?" she asked as she continued to work.

"I don't know," he replied, his voice low as he stepped into the room and closed the door behind him.

She spun around, her eyes wide in surprise. Then she glanced over her shoulder at the uncovered painting on the easel at the other side of the table, and then back at him. A delicate blush climbed up her neck to stain her cheeks.

He followed the direction of her glance to the painting. One black eyebrow rose as his lips twisted into a sardonic smirk. Oddly, he found he could look at the painting with none of the rage he felt when he'd thought of it. He viewed it now as an interesting painting, unconnected to himself. Certainly, he had no memory nor connection to the young man who smiled out at the world without a care, gold eyes gleaming. Had he ever really been that young?

He walked toward the easel.

"I remember that day. My cousins Miles, Sebastian, and I swam in the pond on the Ellinbourne estate. The pond felt bracingly cold as it was fed from the creek that wanders down from the hills at the north edge of the property. That spring and summer had been warm, not at all like the chill spring we now have that threatens our summer crops. One of the cousins was getting married. I don't remember which one. It's a large family. Back then it seemed like every few months someone was getting married, and we all came together at the ancestral pile for those events. The old duke was a big one for family. I think it was Edwin who was wedding that year. He was fifth in line for the title. He was only a year older than me, but already in the military with a commission. He tried to be severe and formidable, but he didn't have the countenance for it. Neither did his twin, Edgar. However, they, like their father, were military men. Napoleon and his bloody war took them away from us," he said bitterly, as he stared at the painting.

"Did you know that Miles, your cousin's fiancé, was actually seventh in line for the title after my grandfather? We've lost a lot of family in the last ten years," he said with a sigh.

"I'm so sorry,"

He shrugged. "There was nothing any of us could do." He turned toward Helena.

"We twitted Edwin for marrying so young while we played. But he was determined. His chosen bride, Sarah Toller, was a good sort. I believe she remarried a couple of years later to a widower with two motherless children."

"Anyway," he continued, "that day, we escaped all the relatives who were arriving. Our Uncle Clarence Wingate joined us. We all thought it a great lark. We had a grand time! That was the last time we had an opportunity for unfettered exuberance, and we made the most of it."

"Your uncle captured that exuberance in your eyes and your carriage," Helena said, standing beside him in front of the picture.

"You think so?" he asked, staring at his face in the painting.

"I do. Look at the light in the eyes. They reflect a smile from within, a character that shone out into the world. Here was a young man who enjoyed life," she said.

"At one time," he acknowledged with a heavy sigh.

"That is all art can give us, a moment in time. However, reminders of these moments are good for us. They teach us hope when life is at its worst."

"It was this painting that led to my greatest disillusionment with my father," he said bitterly.

"Did it really? Or did it just let you see it sooner?" she asked. "And what was sooner? A month, a year? From what you have said, and what my mother has shared about your family, I'd say the rift was bound to happen. Your father's issue stemmed from his life choices, the decisions he made. His second issue was his jealousy over the choices your mother made. You were never an issue. Never you. You were an easy scapegoat, and the painting a sword to pink you with, drawing drops of blood."

"I believed it irritated him that I never tried to wheedle him out of funds."

"Most likely it did. Let me show you something," she said.

She picked up the Holland cover from the floor then draped it around the painting, only revealing his head and upper torso.

"Forget the unclothed condition beneath the cover. What do you see?"

"A picture of a naked me."

"No, you do not. You are not telling me what you see right now. That is what I want to know. Nothing else. I'll tell you what I see. I see a young man with his shirt off. Is he rich or poor? Is he an aristocrat or farm laborer? How do we know?" she asked. "His body is muscular enough for farm labor. Ah, but he is clean. He must be an aristocrat. But wait, his body is glistening. Is that from swimming, or is that sweat? And does the fact that a person went swimming versus honest sweat make a difference as to who he is or where he comes from? Is one or the other better between those choices? And what makes it better?"

"You are making my head spin around," Adam said, laughing slightly, resisting her request to look at the painting differently.

"Good. Maybe that will get your brain functioning again versus being caught in this trough, wading through a miasma of fear."

"Fear?" he pulled his head back. "Why fear? I don't have fear, I have anger," he said.

She canted her head to one side as she looked up at him. "What is the anger?"

"My uncle painted that picture without my permission."

"If your uncle had painted your picture after you had been caught in a rainstorm and were drenched, as you are in this picture, but were clothed, would you be angry?"

"Naturally not."

"So, it is not the permission, it is your unclothed status."

"Yes."

"If I cut the canvas down and reframed it, would you still hate it?"

"I hadn't thought about that. That would depend

how and where it was cut down, I suppose."

"Fair enough," she said, nodding. "It is not your man bits that draw my eyes when I look at this painting, you know."

He frowned at her.

She sighed. "I am an artist, in particular, a sculptress. I speak candidly about the human body. I am not a simpering Miss who pretends to know nothing of men. Which, I suppose—if they have never gone to a gallery or a museum—some could claim innocence. I can't and I don't. I can claim I have never seen the nude male form in the flesh. Whereas male artists might have access to art schools with nude models, a woman does not. Or at least I do not. I believe in Europe they have less of the embarrassment we English have."

He started to smile at her, one corner of his lips twisting upward. "And do you wish to have further acquaintance with a nude male?"

Helena blinked at him. His expression sent a scarlet blush through her.

How did she go from an unemotional artist's forthright discussion about the human body in one moment to a discussion that caused her heart to race and her body to tingle? She looked at the painting in its draped covering, knowing what that covering hid. Her feminine core grew hot. Her eyes met his golden ones watching her. She licked her lips as she felt her pulse throb at the base of her neck.

He did that on purpose!

She'd discomfited him with her frank discussion, now he saw to her discomfort! Oh, she did like this man. But she was not to be so easily conquered. She smiled back at him.

"Touché!" she whispered.

He laughed, the sensual tension between them releasing. He grabbed her in a quick hug, then set her aside.

"Give me a moment. It is not so easy for men to release our desires," he said, turning to look away from her and look out the window, but not before she saw the bulge in his falls.

"Oh!" she said. "Oh! Is this why men and woman do not have anatomy discussions?"

He chuckled. "Partly, yes."

"And here I was thinking—I was thinking—"

"You were thinking what?"

"That you were teasing me," she softly said.

"Helena, I do so love you!"

"What?"

"Marry me."

"But—"

"For real."

"You can't want to marry me. We come from two different backgrounds."

He placed his hands on her shoulders. "So did your parents, and they made it work."

"But why? I am not a society beauty, nor do I have a society woman's talents and attributes."

He shrugged. "I don't need a woman who has musical accomplishments, can speak French, or manage society entertainments, if that is what you mean by talents and attributes. I need a woman who can make me laugh. A woman who can remind me that, despite everything that has happened in the past twelve years, the smiling man in that painting still exists. I need a woman whom I can easily talk with on all manner of subjects, who has a curiosity about life and everything around her, and—importantly—loves animals."

She laughed at the last. "That, I do."

"You do it all. I am comfortable with you. I want a wife I can be comfortable with. Yes, intimacy is important," he said, giving her that sexy eyebrow lift and twist of his lips as his voice deepened.

Helena laughed. Then tears welled in her eyes. "I love how easily we talk and laugh too, and you raise feelings within me I have never felt before that I should like to explore, but it can't be," she said on a soft wail.

"Why ever not, my love?" Adam asked. He pulled her against his chest, stroking her hair.

"My father and mother need me for the factory. I cannot abandon them. My mother readily admits she had no interest in business and my father, well, you have seen for yourself the issues he has. I worry that the stress of the factory will become too much for him and might bring on another apoplexy."

"They have said they are looking for a buyer or another Mr. Bickley."

"Yes, but how long will that take, and will it happen before my father has a turn for the worse?"

Adam wanted to tell her of the plans underway from her parents and his mother, but if her mother had not seen fit to tell her, he could not.

"I want no other woman in my life save you. I will wait for you."

She raised her head from his chest and looked up at him, searching his face. All she saw was love and sincerity. Tears fell freely, sliding down her cheeks.

Adam took his handkerchief from his pocket and blotted her cheeks.

"Everything will work out. Everything," he promised.

He lowered his head to kiss her gently to seal his promise.

CHAPTER 17
EMBEZZLEMENT?

The next day, while Mr. Littledean and Mr. Franklin visited the banker, Mrs. Littledean worked with Miss Velois in the glazing department, and Helena discussed factory management with Mr. Stringer, Adam sat in Mr. Bickley's old office, several account ledgers stacked on the desk by him. Dessie curled up in her dog bed by the office door.

He studied the handwriting of the entries and saw four different people had made entries in the ledgers over the last two months. Earlier ledgers showed one handwriting style, confirmed by Mr. Wallace to be his prior to his accident.

Recent entries had a precise, rounded schoolboy style. Walton confirmed those were his entries. A light, fluid style Helena confirmed as her handwriting. They started upon Mr. Wallace's injury.

The fourth handwriting style started before Mr. Wallace's injury. It matched the handwriting of some color formulae and other documents in the company safe. These were the handwriting entries of Mr. Bickley.

Oddly, they looked like corrections to earlier entries. The entries matched dates and descriptions; however, the earlier recorded dates and amounts recorded by Mr. Wallace were crossed out. The corrections were higher based on the reversal of the two leading numbers. Thus, an entry of 23 S. was corrected to 32 S. And this only occurred where the total was in the 20 to 30 S. range. And the corrections were always up, not down.

Which numbers were correct? The original numbers, or the corrections?

Adam rapped his fingertips against the worn oak desktop.

He rose from his chair behind Mr. Bickley's desk and wandered into the main room, his mind churning.

"Mr. Wallace, these ledgers you gave me are the expense ledgers. Where are the income ledgers?"

"Income ledgers?" Mr. Wallace repeated. He slid off his high stool.

Walton, who sat on the stool across from Mr. Wallace, straightened and looked ready to answer. Adam gripped his shoulder and shook his head slightly. Walton blinked and bit his lip. Adam patted his shoulder.

"Yes, income ledgers," Adam said to Mr. Wallace. "How do you balance profit and loss? Where is that recorded?"

Mr. Wallace's glance nervously slid to another cupboard.

Adam frowned and walked over to the cupboard. "Here?"

"Yes—no!" exclaimed Mr. Wallace as Adam opened the doors.

Adam looked at him.

"They aren't there," he said, wringing his hands together.

"If they are not here, but they are supposed to be, where are they?"

"Mr. Bickley, sir."

"Mr. Bickley is dead."

"Yes, but," he bit his lower lip. "He lent them out," he said, slumping as the words came out in a rush.

"He lent them out?" Adam repeated slowly.

"Yes," Mr. Wallace agreed hurriedly, his head bobbing up and down. He cradled his broken wrist in his other arm. "I argued with him against it. I always kept the books locked, you see, but he was adamant."

He released his broken arm and pulled his handkerchief out of his pocket and dabbed at his perspiring upper lip. "I told him the company's finances should be confidential."

"Was this before or after he began making entries in your expense ledgers?"

"You know about that?" he squeaked.

"It was rather obvious," drawled Adam.

"Yes, I suppose it was." He frowned and shook his head. He compressed his lips tightly, then admitted, "He had some sort of plan to fool Mr. Firkins."

"Mr. Firkins!" The name caught Adam off guard. It wasn't what he expected. Various scenarios swiftly chased each other across his consciousness.

Mr. Wallace nodded. "I told him that was not what he should do. That there wasn't time to set up that kind of deception."

"Deception?" Adam blinked.

The door from the factory courtyard opened, and Helena and Mr. Stringer entered.

Adam frowned and held up a hand, signaling them to wait.

Mr. Wallace dabbed at his upper lip again, then

gestured with the hand holding the handkerchief to the office.

"Might we discuss this privately?" Mr. Wallace squeaked. "In Mr. Bickley's office?" he pleaded.

"What is happening?" Helena demanded, closing the door behind them. "What needs to be discussed privately?"

"The ledgers that aren't here!" Walton said excitedly, his eyes big and round.

Adam closed his eyes briefly. He should have sent Walton away when he started talking to Mr. Wallace.

"The company ledgers aren't here?" She looked up at Adam.

"It seems Mr. Bickley *lent* the ledgers to someone," Adam said drily.

"*Lent?* What?" She walked toward Mr. Wallace; her hands curled into fists. "We suspected something inappropriate was occurring with the ledgers. Were you embezzling from the company and Mr. Bickley caught you?"

Adam thought the fire in her eyes matched the fire in her hair.

"No! No! I swear to you, no!" Mr. Wallace stepped back, stumbling against the high stool behind him. He caught himself against the desk. "It was Bickley! I swear it!"

As much as Adam enjoyed seeing Wallace squirm under Helena's wrath, this didn't get to the root of the issue. He grabbed Helena's shoulders from behind. "I don't think it was Mr. Wallace," he said to her as he pulled her toward him.

She turned her head to look at him over her shoulder."

"What do you mean?"

"Thank you, Mr. Waterbury!" Mr. Wallace said, mopping his forehead and his lip.

"I don't think you are totally innocent," Adam said. "I just don't believe you are the one who *lent*—as you called it—the company ledgers outside the company."

The front door to the office opened. Lord Welbron entered followed by Mr. Littledean and Henry Franklin.

Lord Welbron looked around, an excited, thunderous expression on his face. He raised his arm and pointed at Mr. Stringer.

"George Stringer! I arrest you for the murder of Mr. Charles Bickley!" the magistrate thundered exaltedly.

A stunned silence followed the magistrate's pronouncement.

And George Stringer fainted.

Then the room erupted in voices.

Helena dropped down to her knees by George. "I don't believe it! Walton! Fetch water, please."

Walton jumped off his stool.

"Do you have proof?" Adam asked as the boy ran around him to the courtyard door.

"Yes. And he'll hang!" the magistrate said, kicking at the unconscious man's leg where he lay.

"Stop that!" Helena said furiously.

"What is your proof?" Adam asked

"I have the murder weapon, with his initials on it," crowed the magistrate. And I know why the blackguard did it, too."

From the floor, George started to groan.

Mrs. Littledean and Miss Velois followed Walton back into the office.

"What's happening! Walton said George fainted."

"Maj-tray say Jor kil Bik-ly," Mr. Littledean said.

"Impossible!" Mrs. Littledean said as the magistrate demanded to know what Mr. Littledean said and Miss Velois let loose with a stream of excited French. Dessie started yapping.

"Everyone, stop!" Adam yelled out over the noise. "Mr. Franklin, help Mr. Stringer into Mr. Bickley's office."

"And don't let him out," ordered the magistrate.

Adam scowled at the man and protested, but Helena laid a hand on his arm forestalling him. They wouldn't do Mr. Stringer any good right now. The magistrate was like a horse with the bit between his teeth. There were many aspects to this murder to sort through.

"My lord, how did you come to make this arrest?"

"I don't need to tell you anything."

Adam's eyes narrowed. "Where will you hold him?" he asked instead.

"In the darkest, stinkiest gaol in the county," Lord Welbron swore.

Helena drew in a sharp breath.

"No!" protested Mrs. Littledean and Miss Velois.

"The man is a murderer!" protested Lord Welbron.

"We don't believe he is, and until he goes to trial, he does not deserve that treatment."

The magistrate laughed. "Better accommodations costs."

Adam folded his arms across his chest. "I will make you a wager."

"A wager? What kind of wager?" the magistrate asked.

"The Earl of Norwalk will pay for peerage accommodations for Mr. Stringer. However, if he is proved innocent *before* he goes to trial, you will reimburse the earl double the cost of Mr. Stringer's jail accommodations until the next Quarter Session."

The magistrate laughed. "And if I win?"

"Then the Earl will pay that sum again to you for being wrong."

"What makes you think the Earl will pay up?"

Adam reached into his waistcoat pocket and pulled out his signet ring. "I have the Norwalk signet here. We can use it to seal the wager."

"How do I know that is the Earl's signet?" the magistrate asked suspiciously.

"In the office vault there are letters from the Earl with that seal," Helena offered.

The magistrate smirked. "All right, I'll take that bet, for you will lose. The man is guilty."

"Mr. Smythe, fetch pen and ink, please," Adam instructed.

Walton hurried to get the materials and laid them on the desk.

"I shall write up the rules of the wager for you gentleman to sign," Mrs. Littledean said, using her peerage voice and manner.

Helena smiled.

"When my father was alive, before I married Mr. Littledean, I would do so for my father. I am familiar with the form."

Lord Welbron snorted. "Gambling libertine's daughter, eh?"

She laughed. "Hardly."

"Who were your parents?"

"The Duke and Duchess of Malmsby. And if my mother were here, she'd raise the ante," Helena's mother said calmly as she started writing.

Lord Welbron paused. "Malmsby?" he said suspiciously.

"Yes, my brother, Arthur, is the current duke. My eldest sister's daughter is marrying the Earl of Norwalk's cousin, the Duke of Ellinbourne, so you see how we all know each other. We will be traveling to London for the wedding, of course."

Helena compressed her lips against a laugh. This was unlike her mother, but the magistrate so deserved to be put down.

He visibly swallowed. "Why are you all so sure George Stringer is innocent?" he asked, a twinge of uncertainty coloring his voice.

"What was that you said to us moments ago?" Adam asked. "I believe it was *I don't need to tell you anything.*"

"Here, my lords, I have the document ready for you to sign," Mrs. Littledean said.

Adam picked up the quill. He signed his name, *Adam Waterbury, 4th Earl of Norwalk,* and handed the quill to Lord Welbron.

Lord Welbron's eyes grew large. "But — but—"

"Walton, we'll need sealing wax, please," Adam said.

"Right away, my lord."

CHAPTER 18
REVELATIONS

After Lord Welbron left with his prisoner, Mrs. Littledean proposed everyone come to Tyche Manor, for they had much to discuss.

"This is not a request. It is an order," she said. "I believe we can relax and think clearer away from here. We will close down the factory for the rest of the day, as we did before, with everyone getting payment. I don't trust that the quality of the Littledean work will be up to par with speculation running rife."

Everyone solemnly nodded. Though they enjoyed tweaking the magistrate, they did not ignore the severity·of the mystery. They had a murderer in their midst. That could not be forgotten. Edgy nerves had them wondering what was next.

Adam hired a conveyance from within the city to carry Mr. Wallace, Walton, and himself back to Tyche Manor. Henry went with the others in the Littledean carriage.

No one spoke. It was a solemn group.

Helena sighed as she stared out the carriage window. Last evening, with Adam in her studio, she'd felt she could see her dreams come to life. That they could be more than dreams. She never imagined a man could make her feel the way Adam Waterbury did. That she could feel happy and cherished, the way he made her feel. That she deserved happiness as much as anyone.

And she acknowledged she did. She knew she did deserve that! But deserving and getting were opposite sides of a coin. Life circumstances destroyed the road she would follow, like a flood could wash out a bridge that road traversed.

There it was, over there!

But there was no way to get to that happiness once the bridge washed away.

Her father's apoplexy, Mr. Richmond—the former factory manager—dead of old age. Mr. Bickley murdered, Mr. Humphries fired, Mr. Stringer arrested, and something—she did not know what yet—was going on with Mr. Wallace. It was like some malevolent power strove to destroy Littledean Fine Porcelain, ripping it asunder one slate tile at a time.

Why? To what purpose? How could they get through this? Did they have the strength to rise from the ashes like the legendary Phoenix?

She had to think of her parents. She could not leave this mess in their laps and run off to scoop up her own happiness.

She would ask Adam if she might keep the painting. She could have the canvas cut down and re-stretched if he really hated the entire painting that much. But she needed to see the light in his eyes.

Her eyes started to get teary again. She bit her lip as she willed that weakness away.

~

ADAM WISHED he'd kept Helena by his side. His darling would be thinking of all the reasons they could not find happiness together. If her mother did not tell her the truth of their plans, he would. Why could they not see how committed to them Helena felt she must remain? They were making her miserable, which he was certain was the last thing they wished to do. How could people who loved each other be at such cross purposes?

He looked across from him at his coach companions. Mr. Wallace looked morose, like he was waiting for the hangman's noose. Walton Smythe looked contemplative, like he was working to solve all their problems. Adam wished that were true.

"Walton, what are you thinking about?" he asked, to take his mind off of his own thoughts."

"I've been thinking about Mr. Wallace's arm."

Mr. Wallace rose out of his lethargy. "My arm? Why my arm?"

"I've been trying to figure out how you came to hurt it."

"I fell, I told you I fell," he said irritably.

"I broke my arm when I was five. And I remember when Mr. Gilwray broke his wrist. That were a bad break he had and they worried for infection since the bone came through the skin."

Mr. Wallace begrudgingly nodded. "I remember. He played that injury for as many tankards as sympathy could get him for free."

Walton nodded. "Yes sir. But what I can't figure out is how you came to fall and hurt your arm the way you did. I can see how someone could hit the top of your arm, but I can't see falling. How did you fall?"

"I don't remember," Mr. Wallace said gruffly. "When are you going to Eton?"

Adam recognized Wallace's response as a dodge. He let it go; but considered Walton's observation.

He stared at Mr. Wallace's arm, his eyes narrowing. It made sense. Why hadn't he figured it out before?

"Who did it?" he asked. "Firkins?"

A shudder ran through Mr. Wallace. "No one! I fell, I tell you! I fell. Please, you have to accept that."

"You will be lucky if you can ever use that hand again. Did Dr. Baylor know this was from an attack??"

Mr. Wallace turned his head away. "It will heal. Dr. Baylor promised me."

"And did he promise you will be able to hold a pen properly again?"

Wallace cradled his arm against his chest. He closed his eyes. "We hope so. If—"

"If what?" Adam asked.

"I can't say more!"

"Can't? Or are afraid to? What else did he threaten you with?"

Mr. Wallace turned his head away.

"You're a fool, Wallace," Adam said harshly.

"You don't understand."

"I probably don't. Why don't you tell me?"

Mr. Wallace shifted uncomfortable against the carriage seat. "Not with the boy here."

"Why not?"

"Yes, why not?" Walton echoed pugnaciously.

"That is enough, Walton. I'll handle this."

Walton pouted, but settled into the corner to listen intently.

The carriage left the road and pulled into the tree lined drive before Tyche Manor.

"Mr. Wallace, if you weren't with us right now, I'd say your life is not worth a copper."

He turned his head and looked at Adam. "It was all Bickley's fault," he grumbled.

Adam raised a satyr eyebrow. "We'll continue this discussion inside," he said as the carriage pulled up before the house.

~

WALTON BOUNDED out of the carriage before Adam and Mr. Wallace. As Adam walked into the house he heard Walton shouting "Guess what! Guess what!"

"Mr. Smythe!" Adam yelled.

Walton spun around. "What?"

"Young man, if you wish to be successful in life you need to learn discretion. Starting today."

"But—"

"Enough! Do you wish to be sent home?"

"N-no—"

"What's going on?" Helena asked from the parlor doorway.

"Mr. Smythe is learning that just because he knows something does not mean he can tell everyone else what he knows, exciting as having knowledge and sharing knowledge might be," Adam said.

Helena smiled. "Ah, yes. A hard lesson."

Adam looked back at Walton who stood dejectedly in the middle of the entrance hall. "Mr. Smythe, you will not speak unless invited to speak. Do you understand?"

"Yes, my lord."

Adam looked back at Helena. "Is everyone gathered in the parlor?"

"Yes, and Mr. Sutton is getting refreshments."

Adam nodded. He indicated to Mr. Wallace and

Walton to go before them into the parlor. He stopped at the door by Helena.

"Littledean is in dire management straits," he warned in a whisper.

He knew further problems with factory would drive her further and further from him, that she would be a martyr for her parents. He wanted to warn her, hoping she wouldn't leap to decisions as to what she should do. He was perhaps being selfish wanting her to himself, but his desire was for her happiness as well.

"What?" she asked, looking up at him.

His heart swelled. "Just listen," he requested.

"Like you instructed Walton?"

He smiled and gave a quiet laugh. "Somewhat like that, yes." He touched her back lightly to encourage her to join the others.

Adam walked over to the fireplace where he could easily see everyone in the room.

"We all believe Mr. Stringer to be innocent of killing Mr. Bickley. Now we have to prove it."

"Or you're out a lot of the ready," Walton cheekily piped in.

"Mr. Smythe! What did I tell you out in the hall?"

Walton blanched. "I'm sorry, my lord! Please don't send me away."

"Mr. Smy-eeth, come sit by me," Miss Velois invited, patting the sofa. "If you feel you have to speak, you touch my arm and whisper to me."

Walton jumped up and took her suggestion to sit next to her.

She patted his shoulder.

"Thank you, Miss Velois," Adam said.

She nodded.

Mr. Sutton entered the parlor with the maid to

offer refreshments. The odor of cinnamon cake drifted in the air.

"Hmm, trust cook to know when refreshments need her cinnamon cake," Helena said. "I'm surprised I did not smell it when we came it."

"She baked it this morning, Miss," said the butler. "It was quite fragrant then."

Helena laughed. "I'm sure it was," she said as she accepted a piece from the maid.

When everyone had been served their refreshments and the butler had closed the parlor door behind him, Adam set his cup on the mantel.

"I believe, before his death, Mr. Bickley was being blackmailed. Isn't that true, Mr. Wallace?"

Those gathered in the room all started talking at once. Adam help up his hand to request they stop.

"Mr. Wallace?" he invited.

"Yes, he was," he said, his tone surely.

"Wha—?" Mr. Littledean said.

Mr. Wallace inhaled. "Gambling debts, sir."

"Mr. Bickley, a gambler?" Helena said.

Mr. Wallace nodded. "From London."

"London!"

He rested his elbows on his knees, his expression grim. "When he went to London to visit the showroom."

"I don't understand," Helena said. "I wouldn't have thought gambling to be an interest of Mr. Bickley's."

"It weren't, miss, until his great aunt died and left him forty pounds because she was proud of what he done with his life. Young Firkins overheard him discussing what to do with this Clay Pigeon mates. Told him about a gambling den in London that he couldn't lose at. Told him to let him know next he went to Lon-

don, and he'd introduce him. Said it was so exclusive a
man needed an introduction to enter."

"But if he had invested that money, he'd have been
much better off," Helena said.

Dessie came up to her and pawed her skirts.

"But not quick enough for Mr. Bickley. He was
worried for Mr. Littledean's health. We all were," Mr.
Wallace said.

Miss Velois nodded.

Mr. Littledean shook his head. "I shu—na say
way."

Mrs. Littledean, who sat next to him on the other
sofa, patted his hand. "You thought you were doing
the right thing."

"He wanted to be better off financially so he could
ask for your hand in marriage."

"What!" Helena exclaimed. Dessie pawed at her
again. "In a minute," she said softly to her dog,
pushing her down.

"I thought he was interested in wedding Miss
Velois." Helena said.

"He was; however, he said you were already
wedded to the company, and you'd do anything to protect your parents and he needed to as well. He felt if
you wed, together you would have a better chance to
protect the patronage."

"That doesn't make sense," Helena protested.

"But that is what you have told me," Adam said.

Helena looked up at him, confused as she pushed
Dessie down again.

"You have refused my hand in marriage because of
your concern for the company and your parents."

"No!" Helena denied.

"Helena!" protested her mother.

"You told me your father and mother needed you for the factory and you could not abandon them."

"But—"

"Oh, Helena," said her mother sadly. She looked up at Adam. "You were right, my lord, we should have told her our plans.

"What plans?" Helena asked, looking from her father to her mother.

"To bring on an investor and partner."

Mr. Wallace started to harshly laugh.

"Who?" Helena asked.

"One of Lady Norwalk's protegees."

Helena mouth fell open. She turned and glared up at Adam. "You knew and didn't tell me?"

"I only learned the other day, myself, when your mother told me. I am not involved in my mother's hobby."

Helena's shoulders slumped. Then she stood up. "Come Dessie, I'll take you outside," she said softly, and turned to walk out of the room.

"Helena!" Adam called after her.

"I'll go after her," Mrs. Littledean said, rising from the sofa. "This is my fault. We thought to surprise her. That she would be happy and able to return to her studio."

Miss Velois shook her head sadly as the door closed behind Mrs. Littledean. "Not good to surprise mademoiselle. She care too much, that one."

Adam took in a deep breath. "You are correct, Miss Velois." He turned to Mr. Wallace. "Continue, sir."

"At first Mr. Bickley won."

"Ba —zine," Mr. Littledean said.

"Yes," Adam agreed, "Most likely by design."

"Then he started to lose. A little bit at first."

"Convinced him his luck would turn."

Mr. Wallace nodded. "Mr. Firkins convinced him his luck would turn and gave him the money to continue to gamble."

"When he lost that money and more, Mr. Firkins said he could make it all go away if he would lend him the account books. I refused to give them to Mr. Bickley, that's when he came up with the idea of giving him erroneous account books, but he didn't realize how much time it would take to fake them to make them look legitimate. When Bickley couldn't give Firkins any books, that's when I was visited by Firkin's henchmen. They broke my arm and threatened to do worse. I told Bickley where the keys were."

"Understandably. And I assume they also promised worse if you told anyone."

"Yes," he said despondently. "I am a coward."

"But why murder Mr. Bickley?" Adam asked.

"Sal che—p,"

"They believed you would sell the factory cheap if you didn't have anyone to run it?"

"Wayesh."

"So, no one knew it was really Helena running the factory."

"Much Monsieur Bickley not know about the factory," Miss Velois said with a Gallic shrug. "He know sales, not factory."

"Which is why he did not want to promote Mr. Stringer," Mr. Wallace said.

"He actually wanted to learn?" Adam asked.

"*Oui. Pas un mauvais homme dans son cœur*," said Miss Velois sadly.

"I agree with you, Miss Velois. In his heart, Mr. Bickley was not a bad man. He made bad choices."

"To Mr. Firkins, Bickley was expendable," Mr. Wallace said.

"Lord Welbron said the murder weapon was a knife with Mr. Stringer's initials. Has anyone seen a knife like that in Mr. Stringer's possession?" Adam asked.

"*Mais, oui!*" Miss Velois said.

"Fel-ing nife" said Mr. Littledean.

"What?"

Suddenly Walton on the sofa next to Miss Velois was bouncing up and down and waving his hand. She leaned toward him to have him whisper to her.

"*Oui, mon petit.* A Fettling knife," said Miss Velois.

"What is that?" Adam asked.

"Knife with a blade that bends," she said. "*Un peu.* Removes—umm—seam," she said.

"I think I saw something like that on workbenches in that department."

"Wayesh," said Mr. Littledean.

"So, someone stole one of Mr. Stringer's fettling knives and used it to murder Mr. Bickley," Adam said, mimicking the motion of stabbing downward with the knife.

The others nodded.

Walton started jumping up and down again, waving his hand. Adam signaled him to settle down.

"Left-handed!" Walton blurted out, red-faced.

"Mr. Smythe!" Adam reprimanded. "I told you—"

He stopped, an arrested expression turning from anger to contemplation. "You are right, Walton. If the murderer was facing Mr. Bickley, and Mr. Bickley was stabbed in his neck on the left side of his neck, a right-handed person did it." He looked at the others. "Was Mr. Stringer left-handed?"

CHAPTER 19

A SCULPTORS STRENGTH

Helena grabbed up a handful of her blue muslin skirts and ran across the entrance hall to fling open the front door. Dessie bounded excitedly at her heels.

"Helena!" she heard her mother call after her.

Helena ignored her and ran out of the house without her bonnet or shawl. She ran down the drive until she could no longer hear her mother calling after her, then she slowed her pace to a walk. Her side hurt.

Dessie slowed down, too. Her head down, panting, her pink tongue hanging out.

Helena looked at her exhausted dog and stopped to pick her up.

Dessie gave her one tired lick on her hand then settled herself in the crook of Helena's arm.

Helena patted Dessie's head. "You are a good girl." She scratched behind her ears.

Helena looked up, finally taking in where she was. Sunlight dappled through the tree branches lining the drive. It was warmer this afternoon than it had been so far this year. Was summer finally coming?

She turned her face up to the sun. She didn't worry about the sun bringing freckles, for she already had freckles a plenty. Perspiration glued curls against her head and forehead. She reached up to loosen the top button at her collar.

"I have been so worried about the factory and all the people it supports for so many months now," she said aloud. "Why did they let me worry, so?"

She heard the creak of saddle leather at the same time Dessie did. Dessie yipped and stared into the line of trees along the drive. Helena followed the direction of Dessie's attention. It was Tibault Firkins astride his big bay gelding.

"Mr. Firkins," she said, acknowledging him as she took a step backward.

"You should call me Tibault," he said as he dismounted. "Since we will be married." He tossed the reins around a low tree branch.

"Who says we are going to be married? I distinctly told you no! Besides, you led Mr. Bickley to gambling and to whomever killed him!" she said heatedly, taking another step backward.

"Gambling? Me? My father frowns on gambling. But we will be married. I will control Littledean, and I will make it into something far greater than Firkins Pottery."

Helena planted her hands on her hips. "Have you ever worked a day in Firkins Pottery? You know nothing about pottery," Helena protested.

"I may not have chosen to get my hands dirty in clay and glaze, but you have. Bickley told everyone who would listen how much you knew; how you'd be an asset to anyone taking over the factory. Put you to work and a gentleman would not need to work. As the wife, you would not need to be paid separately. All that appeals to me."

Helena's brow furrowed. "Am I understanding you want to marry me to take revenge on your father, not to get the company for your father?"

"Yes! He has no respect for me. He thinks when we marry, he will gain control of Littledean Fine Porcelain and all its porcelain recipes and glaze formulas, its royal patten and customer list. With that information and his acumen, he believes Firkins Pottery will become more successful than Littledean ever has been, and greater than Wedgwood, Doulton, Spode and the others."

"Wouldn't it be more of a revenge to marry someone outside the industry?" Helena suggested. She slowly bent down to put Dessie on the ground. Dessie sniffed at the horse and Mr. Firkin's boots.

Firkins kicked her away.

"Mr. Firkins!" Helena protested.

"And when we marry, that dog goes!"

Helena planted her hands on her hips. "We are not marrying!"

"Yes, we are, for with control of Littledean I gain access to the highest levels of society. I've thought this out. I get access to all your aristocrat relatives and their friends. They say your father has met Queen Charlotte!"

Helena agreed. "We designed a service for her daughter, Princess Mary's upcoming wedding."

"With those connections, I can rule the pottery industry!"

Helena shrugged slightly as she continued to inch backward. "Customers can discover a new pottery company and patronize them overnight."

Firkins grabbed her wrist. "Where are you going,

Helena? You think I haven't noticed you stepping backward? Thinking of turning to run? I will ruin you so thoroughly that you will beg me to marry you."

"No!" Helena tried to pull out of his grasp. She twisted and turned. "No!" Dessie started yipping. Firkins smacked at the dog, flipping her head over heels. When she stood up, she shook herself. She staccato yipped at him, darting forward to nip at him.

"Dessie, go!" Helena yelled to her dog. "Go get Adam! Go!"

She knew the dog wouldn't understand her; however, Firkins wouldn't know that. If she could rattle his confidence a moment, give him pause, she might get away. Miraculously, Dessie began running back to the house.

"No!" Firkins yelled. He pulled a primed pistol out of his pocket. Helena ran at him as he took aim at Dessie. They fell to the ground as the gun went off, and the little dog ran faster, her ears flying behind her.

Firkins tried to roll on top of her to pin her down. Years of working with heavy clay blocks gave Helena the hidden strength to fight back. Firkins could not control her, but neither could she get away. They wrestled in the dirt. Firkins pulled at her skirts. Helena bucked against him as she grabbed a handful of dirt from beside her head and flung it into his eyes.

"Aargh!"

A shrill whistle pierced the air.

Helena rolled against the horse's legs. The animal jumped, neighing as he came down. Helena rolled backward and the gelding's hooves missed her head, clipping Tibault Firkins' shoulder.

The horse stumbled; Firkins screamed. Helena, tangled in her skirts, scrambled and rolled away as the horse fell sideways, landing on Firkins' leg.

Firkins lay still. Helena and the horse struggled to get to their feet. From behind them Helena heard galloping horse hooves. She turned to see Adam riding bareback down the drive.

Dazed, she stared at him, then at Firkins, and started to laugh hysterically, laughter which swiftly gave way to tears. She stumbled toward Adam as he slid off his horse's back. He caught her up in his arms, gripping her.

She clung to him until the tears turned to hiccups. She lifted her head from Adam's chest and looked up at him. He cupped the back of her head with his hand and leaned down to kiss her. She fought against tears starting anew, but tears of happiness, not the hysterical tears of fear.

When he lifted his head and stared down at her, she said, "We should see to Mr. Firkins."

"Bloody damn, Firkins. He can go to hell. And probably will," he growled before kissing her again.

Behind them came Derek and another groomsman, running.

Adam and Helena broke apart; however, Adam kept his arm around her.

"Mr. Firkins and his horse have met with an accident. Check over the horse to see if he is injured, then fetch the magistrate," Adam grimly told the grooms.

"What about Mr. Firkins?" Derek asked.

Mr. Firkins moaned as he began to regain consciousness.

Adam looked down at the man. "Unfortunately, he's alive. Send someone for Dr. Baylor,"

"Yes, my lord," Derek said. He signaled the other groom to wait there while he returned to the stables.

Adam whistled. It was like the whistle Helena

heard as she fought with Firkins. His horse came trotting up to him.

"You there, what's your name?" Adam asked the groom Derek had stay with Firkins.

"Joseph, my lord."

"Joseph, give me a leg up then hand Miss Littledean up to me."

The groom did as asked, and soon Helena was sitting in front of Adam on the horse's bare back. Together, horse and riders walked slowly back toward the house.

"You're a small woman. How did you fight him off?"

She chuckled. "I handle thirty-pound blocks of clay. I doubt Mr. Firkins has ever picked up a block of clay in his life."

"Hmm. I look forward to the day I can examine those muscles," he solemnly told her.

She smiled as she leaned her head back against him. "As do I."

CHAPTER 20

THE COUNTESS PLAYS
HER HAND

Helena was nigh to screaming in frustration. Ever since Adam had brought her back to the house, someone had coddled and hovered over her, leaving her without a moment to herself—or a moment with Adam.

She granted she had looked horrible when she'd slid off the horse and had then promptly crumpled to the ground. That had had everyone running. But she wasn't hurt. At least she didn't have broken bones as Mr. Firkins had. There were bruises and scrapes and sore muscles, true. Hardly enough to warrant the hovering from the household!

After she'd bathed and been cosseted for over two hours, her mother, the housekeeper, and her maid finally left her in peace.

Helena sighed. Enjoying the quiet.

Almost.

So, who killed Charles Bickley?

Helena paced her room, then decided it was ridiculous that she stay there. She wasn't sick. She wasn't incapacitated. She needed to find out what was going on.

She opened the door to her room and walked down the hall toward the stairs. There were voices in the front hall. She heard Adam's laugh.

"My mother didn't waste any time!"

"She sent me an express the day the Littledeans left Devon," she heard a deep, rough voice say.

Helena started down the stairs. Dessie, who sat at Adam's feet, heard her. She turned, yipped, and ran up the stairs toward her.

"Helena!" Adam called up to her. "What are you doing coming downstairs? You should rest until Dr. Baylor can check you over."

"Nonsense. I'm fine and being driven wild with all the questions revolving in my head. And now here is another one. Who is this gentleman?" she asked as she descended the stairs. She realized as she came down, she wasn't as steady on her feet as she'd thought; but she vowed not to let that show.

"Tobias Grantham, miss," said the blond giant of a man as he bowed, "sent here by Lady Norwalk." He looked like a giant-sized cherub.

"Of the Ingalnook Granthams?" Adam asked.

The man inclined his head. "The same."

"You are a member of Charlotte's *Gentleman's Trade Club*?" Mrs. Littledean asked.

"Yes, madam."

Mrs. Littledean clapped her hands together delightedly. "Excellent! Come into the drawing room, please. I'll get the others since they are here."

"Are you truly feeling well enough?" Adam asked Helena quietly as he led her into the room.

"Yes. I am sore in places, but nothing time won't cure the better for being active."

He led her to one of the sofas and sat down beside

her. He took her hand in his and idly stroked the inside of her wrist with the ball of his thumb. The light, circular strokes sent shivers through Helena's body. She smiled.

"It has been a day for interesting revelations," Mrs. Littledean told everyone. "And another one has just arrived."

The assembly looked from one to another.

"I'd like to introduce you to Mr. Tobias Grantham. Mr. Grantham is well-educated, of good family, but a younger son without a patrimony or the promise of one. He would like to earn one."

There was a buzz of low voices at that last

"For the past five months, he has been working at the London Littledean showroom learning about our customers. With our loss of Mr. Bickley, he has moved here to work directly with us."

The buzz grew louder.

"Aren't you kind of big to work around china?" Walton asked, looking at him askance.

"Mr. Smythe!" Adam chastised.

"Oh, sorry," Walton said, his face scrunched up as he looked at Mr. Grantham.

Tobias Grantham laughed, a deep barrel laugh. "One would think so, looking at my size; however, I assure you, young sir, I have a light touch and outstanding balance. I have not broken a single piece since I've worked in the London showroom. I like beautiful, delicate things," he said, his voice like a deep purr as he spoke about beautiful things.

"What I like, and hope to learn more about, are glazes and finishes. I think we are just learning what we can do on clay, and what we can do with clay. We English have been quite utilitarian with our use of clay. The Germans, the French, and the Italians have opened up our eyes to the artistic aspects of the material."

"Gou, gou!" said Mr. Littledean, his eyes gleaming.

"He might just be the son my father never had!" Helena said quietly to Adam.

"Would that bother you?"

Helena gave the idea a moment of serious consideration. "No," she said slowly. Then she smiled. "I know my father loves me. But he's a man with lots of love in his heart."

"Did you know Mr. Bickley?" Walton asked.

"Yes, I did. And a Mr. Firkins who came into the showroom with Mr. Bickley." He looked at Helena. "He told me he would marry Miss Littledean and I should treat him with respect if I wanted to keep my employment."

"What did you say to him?" asked Mrs. Littledean.

He shook his head. "Nothing. What could I say?"

They heard voices in the entrance hall, then the parlor door burst open, and George Stringer ran into the room.

Everyone jumped to their feet, cries of *"George!" "George!" "Mr. Stringer!"* from everyone. Walton Smythe reached his side first, jumping on him, laughing.

Helena followed Walton and touched Mr. Stringer's arm. "How?" she asked.

Everyone crowded around. Mr. Stringer laughed and cried at the same time. "Thank you, thank you all for believing in me."

Mr. Grantham stood aside. Adam turned to him. "They had arrested Mr. Stringer for Mr. Bickley's murder," he told him. Adam turned back to Mr. Stringer. "Why did Lord Welbron let you go?"

"Young Firkins confessed," Mr. Stringer said.

"Firkins? He had his henchmen who injured Mr. Wallace kill Mr. Bickley?"

Mr. Stringer shook his head. "No, told the magistrate he did it himself."

"What?" Helena exclaimed.

"Why would he kill Mr. Bickley?" Mrs. Littledean asked.

"An wa con-fe?" Mr. Littledean asked.

"Yes," Mrs. Littledean said, nodding. "And why confess?—But come, sit down, everyone sit down," she said.

She rang the bell for Mr. Sutton as everyone got themselves seated again and asked him to bring sherry for all.

"Well, Mr. Stringer?" she said when everyone was settled again.

"It were Lord Welbron's man as told me when he came to release me. He helped get Mr. Firkins to Dr. Baylor. Said Mr. Firkins was screaming his head off that he kilt Mr. Bickley and wanted everyone to know so his father would be disgraced and wouldn't get Littledeans. The magistrate's man told me that at first Lord Welbron wouldn't believe him. That made Mr. Firkins mad, so he described how it happened and that he'd used my knife to throw blame on me to further disrupt the company. That's when Lord Welbron ordered his man to let me go. Said he was right nasty about it, too."

Adam laughed. "That's because I won the bet. One question. You are left-handed, correct?"

Helena laughed and playfully slapped Adam's arm.

EPILOGUE

APRIL 1817, DEVON

The light knock on her studio door roused Helena from her concentration.

"Come in!" she called out. She straightened and picked up a cloth from beside the workbench to rub the worst of the clay off her hands as she turned around. Her back ached. She'd been bent over her clay piece too long.

"Begging your pardon, my lady," said Beasom from her studio doorway. "A crate has arrived for you. Where would you like it?"

"It's here! How wonderful! Please have it brought in here." She dipped her hands into a basin of water she kept on a sideboard and scrubbed the remaining clay off her hands, wiping them dry with another cloth.

She'd had the Mannion estate carpenter build her an easel when she'd received word the painting was done. They'd placed the easel in the room's corner where the painting would benefit from the light coming in the windows without getting direct sunlight on it. She could see it every day as she worked.

She couldn't wait to show Adam.

~

SUNLIGHT STARTED its journey to dusk when the Earl
of Norwalk returned home. In the parlor, where Helena relaxed on the new chaise her husband bought
her, Foster and Dessie lay together in one band of remaining sunlight coming in the tall windows. The big,
male tom cat had adopted the little dog. They were
often together.

Helena laid aside the book she was reading as she
heard her husband's approach. The book was her
cousin's latest publication, a haunting and disturbing
gothic novel. Lancelot had a knack for creating at-
mosphere.

"Beasom said you received a package today," Adam
said as he came into the room.

"Yes!" Helena eagerly said. She threw off the shawl
she'd spread over her legs and rose to her feet to meet
her husband's embrace.

He drew her into his arms, careful not to put too
much pressure against her stomach where their first
child nestled. They expected the babe in two months.
They'd recently finished the new nursery rooms and
were soon to hire a nursery maid.

Helena fairly melted against him. Some days she
could not believe the happiness she felt in her life
with Adam.

When she lifted her head from his broad chest
and stepped back from him, she tucked her hand
in his.

"Come, you must see what came today."

She led him out of the small parlor to the west
wing, where they'd fashioned a studio for Helena's art
in one of the old state rooms. She pushed open the
door.

In the corner stood a large easel covered in a Holland cover, just like she'd had in her studio in Staffordshire.

Adam raised one eyebrow in query.

Helen's smile twinkled up at him as she led him to the covered painting.

She dragged the cover off the painting.

Adam stared at the painting and laughed. He pulled Helena into the circle of his arms as he looked at the artwork.

A carved brass plate on the frame named the work *An Artful Compromise*.

"I approve," Adam said, nodding. "But you did not need to go to such lengths. I have come to terms with the original painting and separated it from my father. This is certainly now a unique painting," he said. "I wonder how your uncle would value it."

"That is a moot point. I will never sell this painting," Helena said vehemently as she stared at the painting, smiling.

The top half was the original *Adam in the Garden of Eden*, but she had not cut the bottom half off as she had once suggested. Instead, it had been altered.

Exotic foliage hid Adam's lower extremities. Now, the young Adam stood among a jungle of leaves and flowers. The vibrancy of color in the repainted parts of the canvas matched the vibrancy of the original sunlit painting.

And best of all, joining the Clarence Wingate signature was a second signature.

Miles Wingate.

SCRIBBLINGS BY HOLLY NEWMAN

Flowers and Thorns Series
    A Grand Gesture
    A Heart in Jeopardy
    Heart's Companion
    Honor's Players

A Chance Inquiry series
    The Waylaid Heart
    Rarer Than Gold
    Heart of a Tiger

The Art of Love series
    An Artful Deceit
    An Artful Compromise
    And coming soon
    An Artful Lie
    An Artful Decision
    An Artful Secret
    An Artful Practice

Other works

Gentleman's Trade
Reckless Hearts
A Lady Follows
The Rocking Horse (novella)
Perchance to Dream (short story)

ABOUT HOLLY NEWMAN

I decided to be a writer when I was in the fifth grade. I filled notebooks with stories—until a mean-spirited high school teacher told me I had no talent for writing. Crushed, for several years I stopped writing, but writing was an itch that wouldn't go away.

My interest in the Regency period came while in high school when I volunteered to re-shelve returned books at the community library. Every week there were Georgette Heyer novels to be shelved. I finally checked one out and became immersed in the world of the Regency.

Fast forward ten years. When attending Science Fiction Conventions, I met people who read science fiction, but also enjoyed the works of Jane Austen and Georgette Heyer, just as I did! They liked these books so much that they wore Regency costumes at the science fiction conventions. They even had Regency era dancing on the convention program. These science fiction readers and writers knew a lot about the Regency era. Intrigued, I did research on the era and quickly went from casual Regency reader to a Regency history buff. Woo-hoo!

After that, with encouragement from science fiction authors, it was just a small step to writing Regencies.

After living thirty years in the Arizona desert, I now live in Florida, seven miles from the Gulf Coast, with my husband, Ken, and our *clowder* of cats. (I don't dare say a number of cats. My husband has developed a habit of collecting strays.)

Subscribe to my newsletter to learn about books and other writings I'm working on. You can sign up here to subscribe and get *Perchance to Dream*, a Georgian fantasy short story.

And be sure to follow me on Bookbub, to be notified about new books and book sales.

Here are other ways to connect!

Website
Facebook
Pinterest
Goodreads

www.ingramcontent.com/pod-product-compliance
Lightning Source LLC
Chambersburg PA
CBHW011514100726
47899CB00010BD/3360